Underneath

Robbie Dorman

Underneath by Robbie Dorman

www.robbiedorman.com

ISBN-13: 978-1-7336388-2-1

Cover design by Bukovero

For my cats.

1

Mary Jensen didn't expect to see the body of the person she replaced, but it waited for her at Research Station Tau.

"It's an emergency," he said. "We need a medic."

She hadn't talked to Mike in a long time, and seeing his name on her phone, calling in the dark, made her hesitate to answer. But she *had* answered.

"Where?" she asked.

"Antarctica," he said, the signal cutting in and out.

"You're in Antarctica? They don't dig for oil down there."

"You're right," he said. "But they do need people to drill through the ice."

"What are you looking for?" she asked.

"Particles," he said. "Invisible. Above my pay grade. You want to come?"

"What happened to the last medic?" she asked.

"Dead," said Mike. "Walked off into the cold."

"Very encouraging," she said.

"It was a fluke," he said. "It'll be good for you."

Hard to argue with that. She had let multiple jobs pass her by, languishing in her apartment in Chicago. Alone. And the pay was great.

She had said yes. They sent paperwork to her inbox in ten minutes and had transport booked within an hour. They wanted her there fast. They had no one else who could handle it, and in the Antarctic, that was trouble.

She had never worked in that kind of cold. The North Atlantic had punished her, but it never got as bad as Antarctica. It stayed cold, even in the summer, and the winter arrived quickly. Probably explained the hurry. Once winter hit, drilling deep would be tough.

Mary looked at herself in the mirror. Her blond hair had gotten unruly over the last several months. She had put off haircuts. She squeezed the extra flesh around her stomach. She had let herself get soft. She buzzed the sides of her head, took a shower, and packed.

She left on an early morning flight to LA, followed by the next available to New Zealand. Mary tried to rest, as tired as she was, but she couldn't. The things Mike had told her bounced off the inside of her skull. And she never could sleep on planes.

The flight to New Zealand felt like eternity, filled with people talking about hobbits. They spoke with passion throughout the eighteen hour trip. She had a feeling in her gut, burrowed deep. Anxiety, excitement, sure, and something else, something she couldn't identify. She tried to read or watch a movie, but she couldn't concentrate. She found herself staring out at the water.

She woke up in a lake of blood. She screamed, screamed and screamed, clutching her belly. The blood followed her, into the car, pooling in the bottom of the wheelchair at the hospital. Greg was yelling for help, yelling for anyone to just do something, all that BLOOD

The pilot jarred her awake with the announcement they were touching down in Auckland. She caught her connection to Christchurch. She would leave for Antarctica the next day. She got a hotel room and slept. She would need all she could get.

She and the other contractors filled the big plane heading to McMurdo Station. She sat near a bookish man, who looked calm and composed.

"Have you been before?" she asked, the five-hour flight underway.

"This is my sixth winter," he said, a small proud smile on his face.

"Sixth?" she said. "You must love the cold."

"I don't mind it," he said. "Still dangerous, though."

"Is it as bad as everyone says?" she asks. "This is my first trip."

"Your mileage may vary," he said. "Some people love it. They like the isolation, the quiet. Are you staying for the winter?"

"I hope not," she said. "I'm on a short contract, to fill in until a research mission is done, hopefully before winter starts. In and out."

"Filling in?" he asked. "What happened to the person you're replacing? Cabin fever?"

"I don't really know," she said. "They walked off, out onto the ice. Found frozen, dead."

"Christ," he said, looking a little aghast. "Do you know why?"

"I didn't get the details," she said. "But they need a medic. Does that kind of thing happen often?"

"Oh no," he said. "It's isolated, so some people turn screwy over the months, but there's always something to do, even if it's just playing board games. It's not sexy. Honestly, it's mostly boring. We all try to keep everyone else safe."

"Makes sense," she said. "Do you know Research Station Tau?"

"Haven't heard of it," he said. "There are dozens of little ones out on the ice, small skeins spread out from McMurdo and the other major stations, but we don't see or hear from each other very often."

"Where will you be?" she asked.

"McMurdo proper," he said. "I handle logistics, taking over from the fellow who does summer contracts. He hates the winter. Works for me."

"So you don't stray from McMurdo?" she asked.

"Ha, no," he said. "It's isolated enough, and there's a few hundred people there. I can't imagine going out farther. It's a different world out there. Reminds you of how small we are, how weak we are." He looked at her. "I'm sorry, I don't want to give you the wrong impression. The Antarctic is dangerous, but if you're a field medic, you've seen places just as bad. It's not the cold that will you get you, it's the isolation. It takes a long time to get help, and the farther out you go, the longer it takes. The weather is unpredictable, and if you're bleeding out on one of the stations, it'll be hours or days before transport gets to you. It's my job, so I know."

"So don't bleed out," she said. "Got it. I'll do my best."

"How'd you get the job?"

"Through an ex," she said.

"Oh man," he said, cracking a smile. "Hope you're on good terms."

"Could be worse," she said.

"That should be the motto of the entire continent," he said.

The water didn't change until it did, small shreds of ice drifting through the ocean. And then she saw it, the land itself, a huge plane of white. It looked incredible. And foreboding.

"There it is," said John, her airplane friend. "It's a beaut."

They skirted the coast, Mary marveling at the endless cascading plateaus, hills, crags, ice and snow, an infinite field of frozen land.

"It never ends," she said.

"Big as Australia," he said. "No one realizes how huge it is until they get here."

She saw McMurdo Station from the air. She didn't know what she'd expected. A few clusters of buildings on the southern tip of Ross Island stuck up out of the mud and frost. The airplane passed it and touched down on the sea ice runway, frozen over again as the temperatures dropped. The plane skidded to a halt and they got out.

"Good luck," said John. "And don't be afraid to call for help if you need it. We're all we have out here."

She walked through McMurdo Station. It didn't take long. It looked like a small mining town, one whose population had dwindled as winter approached. She knew it had a capable hospital. It supplied all the nearby stations, including Tau.

She didn't have time to linger. The ride out to Tau waited for her. The weather had cleared, and it wouldn't last long.

She met the welcome wagon at McMurdo, and then she boarded the helicopter, a big one, flying out a few hours to Tau. She waited alone near the chopper until the pilot arrived. She sat passenger with her, headset on.

"You ever been on the ice before?" she asked. Calm, cool, collected. Just another flight for her.

"My first time," said Mary.

"A virgin!" said the pilot. "And you're going out this far?"

"It's the job," said Mary.

"I hear ya," said the pilot. "I'm Alex."

"Mary."

"Nice to meet ya," she said. "Weather hasn't been this good in months. It cleared up for you."

"How often can you fly?"

"It varies," said Alex. "Never predictable. So we go where we can, when we can. Still beats the service."

"Where'd you serve?"

"Marines. Iraq," said Alex, her eyes always forward, scanning the wide open horizon of white.

"Oorah," said Mary. "Afghanistan. Semper fi."

"Semper fi," said Alex. "You've seen some shit, then. This place'll kill ya, just the same."

"You ever hear of people just walking out onto the ice?" asked Mary.

"What do ya mean?"

"The person I'm replacing. One day he walked out into the cold. Died."

"Never heard of that," said Alex. "But you see a bunch of weird crap out here. People go bug-eyed, cabin fever, all that. Psych evals can only show so much. He mighta just wanted to die, and thought that was the easiest way. He musta been crazy, though, because if I'm choosing how I die, the cold ain't it."

"My dad always told me you went numb," said Mary.

"Yeah, I guess, eventually," said Alex. "But that's any way, if it's slow enough. The cold burns, just like fire, burns and aches at the same time. I've pulled people off the ice, rescue situations. It hurts you, every part of you, all at once."

"Everyone loves talking about the cold down here," said Mary.

"It's always there," said Alex. "It becomes everything."

They settled into an easy silence with the helicopter whirring above them. Mary found it hard to mark her progress with no landmarks. The icy interstitial planes blended together, cut apart by mountains and hills. Every new plateau stunned her with its beauty.

"Pretty," said Mary.

"No doubt," said Alex. "But eventually, you see the other side of it. Get tired of it."

"I hope I'm not here that long," said Mary. "In and out, before winter hits."

"Good luck with that," said Alex. "No plan survives contact with enemy."

"What's the enemy out here?" asked Mary. "The cold?"

Alex laughed at that. "No. Everything."

After a couple hours in the chopper, a speck of black appeared on the horizon. As it got closer, Mary saw it. Research Station Tau. The dark buildings stood out in the vast plain of white.

"That's it," said Alex. "Tau."

She touched down on the ice a hundred yards from the compound. She turned off the helicopter, the engine winding down.

"I'll follow you in," said Alex. "I've got a pickup."

Mary grabbed her bags and crunched across the hard surface, temperatures in the negative teens. Her watch read 6PM Chicago time, four days after she left. Or was it three? Or five? She didn't know. The cold cut through her, the lost sleep and constant travel shifting her perspective.

A small, pear-shaped figure waited for them, obscured by parkas and extreme weather gear. The wind pushed past them, but nothing serious. Mary knew it got worse in the winter.

"Hi," said the figure, waving. "I'm Dr. Darrow, but you can call me Helena. Let's get you inside."

They all lumped into the cramped room, shaking off as much snow as they could. Mary felt immediate relief, the thick insulation of the habitat closing out the cold. She could breathe again.

"Where's my pickup?" asked Alex. "I'd like to head back ASAP."

"Of course," said Helena. "We didn't know exactly what to do with him, so we put him in the freezer."

They walked through a few greenish corridors and came to a door marked FREEZER in big stencil letters. Helena opened it with her key, and they entered. Foodstuffs filled half the room. By the near wall lay a black body bag. Mary recognized it immediately.

The sight of dead bodies didn't affect Mary much, not after two tours in Afghanistan and the oil rigs. She'd watched men die.

But she had never seen the corpse of the person she was replacing, not in her civilian life. The reason she was here, frozen like a side of beef. Bagged and ready to go.

"Can I get some help?" asked Alex, taking one end of the bundle, tied to a spinal board. Mary grabbed the other side, her first official duty as the Tau medic. She helped Alex back out to the chopper, loading the dead man in the storage compartment.

"Good luck out here," said Alex. She strapped him down, and left. Helena watched them from outside the entrance. Mary rejoined her, and they returned inside.

Helena uncovered her face, unwrapping layers of scarves, revealing a small forced smile. Her black hair spilled out of her beanie. She pulled off a glove, offering a handshake to Mary. Mary did the same, their cold hands touching.

"Welcome to Tau."

2

Helena took Mary to her room first, filled only with a bed, closet, and footlocker.

"It's not very big," said Helena. "But none of them are. There's not a lot of space to go around. All the bedrooms are in this corridor, except for Dr. Schuller's, which is attached to his lab. I'm right next door."

Mary dropped off her stuff, and Helena gave her the grand tour.

"There are only four buildings at Tau, this one being by far the largest. It holds sleeping quarters, bathrooms, the kitchen and mess hall, the communal living space, and several labs. When not on the dig site, it's where we spend all of our time."

They walked past empty bedrooms, doors shut. Helena

led her into the mess hall, consisting of a handful of long tables with benches set up. Noises came from the kitchen.

"Bill, you in there?" asked Helena, shouting into the kitchen, full of stainless steel.

"You don't got to yell at me, Helena," said Bill, a big, barrel chested man, dressed in flannel and blue jeans, his sleeves rolled up, a bandanna holding back a wild head of brick-colored hair, a hair net corralling a bushy beard. "I ain't hard of hearing. At least, I wasn't." He leaned in towards Helena, nudging her.

"Oh, whatever," she said. "This is Bill. You and him make up the entirety of our support staff. Bill cooks, cleans, and does whatever else needs doing around here."

"I wear many hats," he said, his crunchy drawl filling the room. "Nice to meet you, Dr. Jensen."

"Ha, I'm not a doctor," said Mary. "Just a medic. Enough to be dangerous."

"Well that suits me fine," said Bill, smiling. "We got enough doctors around here, if you know what I'm saying."

"What exactly are you saying, Mr. Norris?" asked Helena.

"Oh, nothing," said Bill, nudging her again. "I love doctors, especially when I'm surrounded by them for months on end, always correcting me."

"You thought shrimp and crab were the same animal," said Helena.

"I still ain't convinced they're not," said Bill. "Despite all that talking you did to me about shells and salt water. Makes no difference to me. Both are tasty, and we have neither of them to eat anymore."

"I think we can move on from the kitchen. I'm sure Bill

has plenty of work to do," said Helena.

"I see how it is," he said. "Miss Mary, what's your favorite dessert?"

"I like everything," said Mary. "I like peach cobbler a lot."

"I can do that. I try and make everyone's favorite, at least once."

They continued on the tour, the communal living space up next. Couches, love seats, and recliners all sat near a projector. She saw some video game consoles piled in the small entertainment center. A pool table dominated the area, with a bookcase on the wall filled with movies and a few board games.

"We try to keep things light. We have movie nights, board game nights, pool tournaments, you know," said Helena. "But lately, everyone's been so busy, we just haven't had the energy. We're supposed to be out of here by winter."

"Is everything on schedule?" asked Mary. "I'm sure losing your medic wasn't part of the plan."

"It wasn't," said Helena. "I hate to even think about it. We should finish in time, but we're all getting nervous, especially Dr. Schuller. I still think we'll make it with some time to spare. Half the crew is out at the dig site now, working hard, trying to hit depth before winter comes and demands payment."

They stopped in at one lab, full of stacks of papers, whiteboards, and equipment that Mary didn't recognize.

"This is the physics lab," said Mary. "Jane and Andrew are working at the dig site, but this is their lab."

They proceeded on to another room. Paper littered the tables. A row of freezers lined one wall. A man in a plaid button down and a lab coat stared at a microscope and then consulted a notebook in front of him. A mop of curly auburn hair flopped around as he moved.

"And this is where I work. I share it with Jim," she said. "Say hello, Jim."

"Hello, Jim," he said, smiling. He reached out his hand. "Jim McTaggart."

"Mary Jensen," she said, shaking it.

"You must be our new band aid specialist," he said.

"I hope it doesn't go beyond that," she said.

"I hope so too," said Jim. "I wasn't expecting Steve to jump off the deep end. He was as steady as a rock."

"Do we have to talk about it?" asked Helena.

"We're gonna have to discuss it sometime," said Jim. "I'm sure Mary wants to know why she came out here in the first place."

"Dr. Schuller can handle it," said Helena, trying to change the subject. "Jim is a glaciologist."

"I study ice," he said. "And all contained within. While Helena here is a physicist. You can't even see what she studies. One point, Jim."

"That's a little dismissive," said Helena.

"I'm just teasing," said Jim. "Where would be without you?"

"Probably not freezing our butts off," said Helena.

"Helena is the reason we're in this spot in the first place," he said. "She was able to pinpoint the location of the particles, with Dr. Schuller."

"I didn't do much," said Helena, blushing. "It was mostly Dr. Schuller."

"You're friends with Mike?" asked Jim.

She didn't know how to answer. Her face betrayed her

because Jim immediately changed the subject.

"I'll ask a different question. Do you play poker?" he asked.

"I like it more than it likes me," she said.

"Perfect," he said, smiling. "That's who we need in our poker game."

"Goodbye, Jim," said Helena, ushering Mary away.

"Jim is very nice," she said. "Not a mean bone in his body. He's good to have here, always keeps the peace."

"Is that a problem?" asked Mary. "Keeping the peace?"

"Everyone mostly gets along," said Helena. "But in such a small space, with nowhere to go except out in the cold, sometimes people's tempers get the better of them. Jim makes sure cooler heads prevail."

"Anything else to see in here?" asked Mary.

"Not really," said Helena. "There are three other buildings. One is the garage, where the tractors are stored, along with extra drilling equipment. We don't need to go in there. The other is the generator building, where all of them are kept, and all the gas and everything."

"You said there were four buildings?" asked Mary.

"Yes," she said. "And that's where we'll end our little tour. Dr. Schuller's office and personal lab. He stayed behind today to greet you."

"Should I grab my parka?" asked Mary.

"It's only a short walk," said Helena. "I usually don't. It's less than a minute outside."

Mary regretted her decision not to gear up almost immediately. She saw Schuller's office as soon as they stepped out, less than a hundred feet away. Without her thick parka, the wind and cold cut right through her, down to the bone.

They hustled through the chill, the fog of their breath being carried away by the air before they could see it. Helena led the way. It took less than a minute, but it felt like an hour. Helena knocked and entered, not waiting for a response.

The warmth greeted them, cooler than the main building, but still much warmer than outside. The door opened into a small antechamber, and then Schuller's lab and office. This room was the biggest yet. Perks of being the boss. There were a few tables, with more paper, more notebooks, and more equipment. More freezers along the wall. A desk sat in the corner with a multi-monitor setup on top of it, presumably Schuller's computer.

Dr. Schuller emerged from the room attached, which Mary guessed what his bedroom. He had a nervous energy about him, his hands always moving, steepling against himself, or anything nearby. He stood as tall as Mary, but slender, as if a slight breeze would blow him away. He was balding, a slim horseshoe pattern of hair still hanging on, light and wispy. He wore glasses, thin and almost invisible. He smiled when he saw them.

"Helena," he said. "I'm glad to see you. This is Mary, I presume."

"Yes," said Helena, suddenly less talkative. "Mary Jensen, this is Dr. Ian Schuller, lead at Research Station Tau."

He reached out a slim hand, and Mary took it. It felt cold in the warm room, even though her own hands were chilled from being outside.

"Welcome aboard, Ms. Jensen," he said. "Glad to have you. We were flying without a safety net for a few days there."

"Glad to be here," said Mary.

"Helena has shown you around?" asked Schuller.

"Showed you your accommodations?"

"Yes," said Mary. "She's been very helpful."

"Great, great," said Schuller, his fingers still moving. "Would you mind leaving us, Helena? I'd like to talk to Mary about our mission and the research. Onboarding, so to speak."

"Of course, Dr. Schuller," she said, with a quick glance at Mary, before leaving back into the cold. A frigid burst of air flew into the room.

"Please, Ms. Jensen," he said, gesturing to a chair. "Have a few minutes to chat? I can fill you in on what we're doing here and answer any questions you might have."

"Sure," she said, sitting down.

"What do you know about our research?" asked Schuller, behind his desk. "Mike Hale recommended you, correct? What did he tell you?"

"Not much," she said. "It's been a whirlwind getting down here, and he only told me something about drilling into the ice. Other than that, I don't know. You have physicists, geologists, glaciologists, and a team of drillers."

"Yes," said Schuller. "All important in their own way. And yes, what we are looking for is down in the ice."

"Mike mentioned invisible particles, but that doesn't mean much to me," said Mary.

"Well, he's not wrong," said Schuller, his smile disappearing. "But it is a vast oversimplification. We're searching for the origins of humanity."

"And it's down there in the ice?" asked Mary.

"I think so," said Schuller. "Deep, deep ice, frozen for hundreds of thousands, if not millions of years. Inaccessible, impossible to reach. Until now."

"Why now?" asked Mary.

"Climate change. Global warming. It is opening up the permafrost. Most unfortunate, but there is a bright side, and it is allowing our mission to happen. Allowing us to dig deeper, into older ice, and unbury what the cold buried long ago."

"What do you need from me?" asked Mary.

"To do your job," said Schuller. "And keep a level head. The cold and the drills are both dangerous, along with the hundreds of other mundane things that can cause injuries. Help our team, take care of them, and you'll be here to witness something truly remarkable."

"What happened to the last medic?" asked Mary. "Why did he go out on the ice?"

"I don't know," said Schuller. "He had shown no signs of instability, as far as I can tell. Sometimes, people just snap. Here one moment, gone the next. And he took his own life, here, rather than wait until he was back in civilization. A selfish act, especially out here. He left us with no one with any medical knowledge, or experience. It could have led to other deaths—"

"I'm here now," said Mary. "And I'll take care of everyone as best I can."

"That's good to hear," said Schuller. "Mike spoke highly of you. Of your military service, of working out on the oil rigs. Rough environments. It's why I fast-tracked your arrival, pulled the few strings I could. You're the kind of person we need out here. Someone who will do what it takes."

"And you think we'll find the origins of humanity down there?" asked Mary.

"That is my hypothesis," he said, his eyes wide, excited.

"We still don't know how we came to be, Ms. Jensen. How we rose up off of four legs, and became the dominant form of life on the planet, rising into the civilization we are today. Evolution, you might say. Simple evolution. But that explanation never sat well with me. Is that all we are? Is a few fortunate mutations all that differentiates us from chimps? Where is the spark?"

His eyes glowed with a fervor as he spoke. He *believed*.

"I am an atheist," he said. "I have been as long as I could reason, but it is the one aspect of religion that I always appreciated, the divine spark, the uniqueness that sets us apart, that led to us exploring space and left chimps tooling around in the dirt. And I think that spark is down in this ice. That, down there, is the closest thing we'll ever get to a higher power."

His hands were up now, clasped.

"We will find God."

3

Everyone crowded into the small mess hall after they got back from the dig site. It smelled amazing. Bill served biscuits and gravy from the kitchen. The whole station ate happily, with Mike and Schuller notably absent.

The main clump of people sat around two tables, right next to each other. Four sat together, two men and a woman, and Jim, the scientist she had met earlier. They laughed at something, voices loud, back and forth.

Mary went to the counter to get some grub.

"Smells great, Bill," she said, Bill turning, preparing dinner for her. He laid down two biscuits cut in half and covered them in sawmill gravy. Her stomach rumbled. She realized her last meal had been twelve hours ago, two protein bars shoveled down at McMurdo.

"Thank you very much, Miss Mary," he said, handing over her plate. Mary leaned closer to the counter.

"Who should I sit with?" she asked, her voice low.

"The bigger group, thems all the roughnecks, aside from Jim, who everyone likes," answered Bill, talking out of the side of his mouth. "The other two, both doctors. Jane and Andrew, they're alright, but not friendly types. Reckon you're more of a roughneck type, 'specially if you know Mike."

Mary winked, and took her plate to the larger group, sitting in the empty spot next to Jim. Jim smiled at her as she sat down, in the middle of a conversation.

"So, I'm on the phone with my girlfriend at the time, breaking up with her," said Jim, smiling.

"Over the phone?" asked the other woman at the table, blond hair and blue eyes, as big as any of the men, her shoulders broad and strong. "Rude."

"I was in college," he said. "And absolutely terrified of her. Anyways, I was on the phone, trying to break up with my girlfriend at the time, and I hear knocking at my bedroom door. I was sharing the house with three other dudes, so I assumed it was one of them, wanting to play Halo or something, so I just yelled 'PHONE', and kept trying to break up with my girlfriend. But they kept knocking, so I ignored them. Then I hear the key in the lock, so I turn back around."

"Your roommates had the key to your room?" asked one of the other dudes, a young kid, clean-shaven, stocky with strawberry blond hair. He had a black eye and a midwestern accent.

"One of them was subleasing to the rest of us, so he had

keys to everything," said Jim. "For emergencies, he said. So I turn around, about to tell him how it wasn't cool to just let himself in when I'm on the phone, but it's not my room-mate."

"Who was it?" asked the amazon.

"It was the cops," said Jim. "Three of them, guns drawn."

"Oh shit," said the other dude, shorter than the man and woman, with black hair and a goatee. Mary could see the cords in his neck.

"And I'm still on the phone with my girlfriend," said Jim. "And so I was trying to build up to the breakup, saying how I wasn't happy, etcetera, but then the cops were there, with their guns on me. So everything else came out in a long string of soIthinkitsbetterifweseeeotherpeoplecopsarehere, gotta go, bye, and I dropped the phone."

Everyone burst out in laughter, Mary included.

"So what happened with the cops?" asked Mary.

"So, I drove a white car at the time," said Jim. "An old Chrysler. And they had asked my roommate, does Jim live here, and does he drive a white car?"

"And he narced on you," said the black-haired dude.

"He did," said Jim. "But I don't blame him. These were sheriff officers, not city cops, and they did not play, consid-ering the amount of meth labs in our neighborhood. But the house was on a long dirt driveway that we shared with a few other houses, and in one of those other houses, there was another Jim, who also drove a white car, and also happened to run a meth lab."

"So they thought you were meth Jim," said the young kid.

"So I turned around, broke up with my girlfriend, dropped the phone, and the cops saw my face and immediately knew I wasn't the guy they were looking for. So they left. And I walked outside and there were a dozen cop cars out there. They really wanted Jim in the white car. And as they're about to leave, guess who comes driving down the road?"

"The other Jim in the white car?" said the amazon.

"Bingo," he said. "So they got their man, and I broke up with my girlfriend."

"You didn't call her back?" asked Mary. "That's terrible."

"I repeat," said Jim. "I was terrified of her. So the cops did me a favor."

Everyone laughed again. Jim took the moment of silence afterward to introduce Mary. The amazon's name was Beth, the young guy was Bart, and the black-haired dude was Teddy.

"You old friends with Mike?" asked Beth.

"I worked with him on a rig, in the North Atlantic," said Mary.

"He mentions you a lot," said Beth.

"Does he now?" asked Mary.

"He does," said Beth. "Said you saved his life once or twice."

"He's a goddamn liar," said Mary, smiling. "It was way more than once or twice."

Everyone laughed again.

"Speak of the devil," said Jim, motioning with his head. Mike walked into the mess hall, the same mountain that towered over everyone else. With umber brown skin, he wore a long sleeve henley and heavy work pants. He glowered, his fair features angry at something. Mary hadn't seen him in over five years, but he looked the same, same as the day he had left.

Mike grabbed his dinner from Bill and sat down with them. He looked down at his food, not even seeing Mary. He ate without saying a word.

"What's wrong?" asked Beth.

Mike still didn't look up. "Schuller," he said.

"Use your words," said Jim.

"I swear, Schuller cares more about those particles down in the ice than any person alive. One day, I'm going to—"

And he looked up, and saw Mary.

"Hey," she said. "You should focus on either biscuits or the yelling. Wasting a good meal with all that anger."

"Mary," he said, and stood up. He walked around the table and hugged her, his big arms wrapping around her. She hugged him back, his embrace warm.

"I'm glad you're here," he said, in her ear. He let go and moved back around to the other side of the table. She lingered there for a second and then sat down.

"I was arguing with Schuller," said Mike. "I won't be pushed any harder."

"What was it this time?" asked Bart.

"He wants us at the drill site for longer hours," said Mike.

"Horseshit," said Teddy, immediately.

"I told him," said Mike. "We work any harder, and there'll be more injuries, and productivity will go down. He doesn't understand. He just wants to hit depth, damn the human cost."

"He's worried about making it on time," said Jim. "If we don't see results this season, it's a wasted year."

"I know," said Mike. "But no one's life is worth that, and the longer we work, the more tired we get, the more dangerous everything is. And right after we lost Steve."

"Everyone told me it was suicide," said Mary.

"Everyone has a breaking point," said Mike. "You know that. Steve reached his. I don't blame him for that. He was looking out for all of us and—"

And then Helena appeared in the mess hall, blood dripping off the end of her arm. She held a blood-soaked paper towel against it.

"Mary? I need some help."

*

Mary cleaned the wound, a long gash in Helena's forearm, wiping away the blood as it welled up out of her skin.

"How did this happen?" asked Mary.

"I was working on an ice sample in Dr. Schuller's lab, and I must have stopped focusing, or glanced away, and the saw slipped," said Helena. "It's my fault. I should have been paying more attention."

Mary stabbed a syringe into some local anesthetic, injecting it near the cut. Helena winced.

"Ooh, that's cold," she said. "Will I need stitches?"

Mary looked at Helena, and she was looking away.

"Have you seen it yet?" asked Mary.

"I couldn't," said Helena. "I saw the blood, and I was too afraid."

"Then don't look," said Mary. "But you definitely need stitches. Are you ready? You'll feel some pressure."

"Y—yes," said Helena, breathing deeply.

Mary started, sliding the needle and thread through Helena's skin, sealing the wound. Mary worked fast, out of habit. In and out, in and out. Mary worried that Helena would black out, but Helena stayed conscious. Her other hand gripped the bench.

She finished. Fourteen stitches.

"Alright," said Mary. "You're good."

"Should I look?" asked Helena.

"I think you should," said Mary. "As long as you won't faint."

"I won't," said Helena, and looked over at the line of stitches keeping the wound closed. "Pheeeeewwwwww." She breathed out, letting air out in a slow, steady stream. "Ok. That's enough."

Mary bandaged it, wrapping the non-stick gauze in surgical tape.

"You're ready," said Mary. "Try not to itch. I'll look at it again in two weeks, hopefully the stitches can come out then."

"I hope so," said Helena.

"And try and be more careful," said Mary. Helena got up to leave and then stumbled, almost falling over. Mary caught her and sat her back down.

"How much sleep have you been getting?" asked Mary.

"I don't know," said Helena. "Three to four hours a night, maybe?"

"That's not enough," said Mary. "Get rest. That's an order."

"There's too much to do," said Helena. "And not enough time. Dr. Schuller—"

"If you pass out on the ice," said Mary. "You won't be doing any work at all, and someone else will have to carry you back in. Sleep. If Schuller says anything different, you tell him to talk to me. This isn't a negotiation. When it comes to medicine here, I'm the boss. Understand?"

"Yes," said Helena. "I'm sorry."

"Don't apologize," said Mary. "Get some sleep."

Helena left, more steady on her feet. A sliver of unease entered Mary's mind. She had only just set up her office and examination room today. A computer sat in the corner, but it was empty, aside from the barest of touches from Steve.

She hadn't looked in the filing cabinet yet. She opened it and found multiple file folders sitting inside. Mary pulled out everything, a six inch stack on her desk. She worked through them, a folder for everyone at the station, with their complete medical records.

Most of them didn't surprise her. The roughnecks all had histories of broken bones and strained ligaments. Mike tore his ACL eight years ago, with reconstructive surgery following. She had helped him with that one. He worked months with it torn, dragging his leg behind him as he muscled drilling equipment into place.

Beth broke her back four years ago. Bart, being so young, had the fewest injuries, only some sprains and scars. Teddy had fractured both his ankles once upon a time. They had faced extraordinary conditions, so their injury history didn't shock her. All had passed their physicals. The science team's medical histories were much more mundane, aside from a broken arm Jim seemed to suffer sometime in college. Considering the story she heard from him earlier in the evening, that didn't surprise her either.

The folders also contained their psych evaluations, with reports on how they responded to pressure and isolation. She took them with a grain of salt. She had been in the shit, under fire. And whatever you knew about that person before, none of it bore out once it was on. The calmest, coolest motherfucker alive could bug out the moment they were under pressure, and a neurotic mess could turn into Clint Eastwood.

She looked at Schuller's file last, and took particular care. His physical showed nothing wrong, no past injury, no medication. Healthy as a horse.

She turned to his psyche eval, done prior to shipping out. She read through it. Completely mundane. Suffered from headaches when stressed, but most people did. May shut down in pressure situations. No history of mental breakdown.

Wait. This looked familiar. She flipped back through the other evals, one by one. She found the discrepancy. Schuller's report matched Helena's. Word for word, except for the primary information.

She looked back at Schuller's report, closer now, at every field. She could spot the artifacts, when they copied it. Someone had replaced Schuller's original with this.

Multiple questions popped into Mary's mind, but they were immaterial. Somebody tried to replace Schuller's eval, or cover up that he never got one in the first place. Either Steve, or Schuller himself.

Only one question of substance remained.

Did Steve walk out on the ice on his own?

Or was he forced out there, because of what he knew?

4

"I drive out myself whenever I can," said Schuller, behind the wheel of the tractor. "It feels incredible to traverse terrain that no man has ever set foot upon. See things no person has ever seen, except for us, right now."

She didn't choose Schuller as her personal chauffeur but here she was, alone with him in the huge vehicle. They churned their way across the ice on their way to the dig site. Everyone else headed out early this morning, leaving her behind to sleep. Helena still slept in her room when Mary got up. She found Schuller waiting for her in her office. She needed to see the dig site, he said, to truly understand.

And so they crawled across the ice. The tractor made its way to the dig site two miles from the main camp. The machine ambled. Because of its massive size, it had multiple safeguards so it wouldn't get stuck in the ice. Mary felt warm in the tractor's cabin, warmer than she'd been since she left New Zealand.

After her discovery of the forged psyche eval, she wasn't getting a better chance to observe Schuller. Leading questions wouldn't work on someone of his intelligence. She needed to be patient and careful. Maybe not that patient. Schuller *never* stopped talking.

"Just think," said Schuller. "Every peak, every plain, every meter of ice and snow, hasn't been seen or marked by humanity. Every second, everything we touch, we make history. It's an incredible place. Our very presence is momentous. To think, we reach for the stars, when there are still places on Earth we haven't tasted."

As he talked, his hands danced across the massive steering wheel, fingers tapping, pointing, pounding on the leather. The vehicle listed as he got distracted. He pulled it slowly back onto the deep tracks laid down by the tractors over months.

Mary tried to listen to Schuller, but the surrounding environment made it difficult. The perspective from above had destroyed Mary's sense of scale. At ground level, the mountains and hills of ice surrounded them, rising above them. The long rippling plains stretched out in front of them. They saw for miles in any direction until the wind ripped through and pulled particles of ice into the air.

The environment inspired beauty and terror in kind. Out here, the isolation sunk in. Inside the main camp, you could be tricked by the warmth, the company, the access to food and water, to your bed. Out on the ice, Mary couldn't mistake how alone they were. Help wouldn't come for hours or days, depending on the weather. And as the tractor crawled along on its inexorable track to the dig site, it emphasized how reliant they were on these machines. If they broke down, it would be a long walk back, through frigid cold. Even with all their extreme cold clothes, they would die quickly, as temperatures dipped down into the high negatives. Being outside would be an assured death.

"Isn't this wonderful?" he asked.

"It's something," said Mary, staring out the window.

"It holds such secrets," he said. "And such excitement."

Schuller didn't fake his enthusiasm. His eyes gleamed, his fingers tapping.

"I heard about the other doctor's specialties," said Mary. "But I didn't hear yours. What did you study?"

"If you're asking about degrees, I have a doctorate in geology and physics, but I find the confinement of academic life tiring," he said. "I've focused mostly on interdisciplinary applications of my studies since then. They haven't always paid off, but I find that work much more exciting than working in only one field. You'll see that reflected in my team. I don't like unitaskers. I want people who can do anything, who wear many hats, as our colorful cook is wont to say. Jacks of all trades."

"Masters of none," said Mary.

"Ah, that's where you're wrong, Ms. Jensen," he said. "That saying was used to bring men down who mastered multiple fields, the renaissance men like Da Vinci. Polymaths who created masterful art, invented technology, researched science, all in a single lifetime. They didn't confine themselves to a a particular field. Why should I?"

The tractor weaved back and forth as he spoke, losing

focus on his driving. Her fingers gripped the seat.

"This gets me so excited," he said. "This is real science, not the labs or offices back in civilization. Out here in the true wild, this is where the real discoveries are made. Every single trip out here, we could be redefining the origin of man. Our names would be alongside Darwin. I can feel it, in the air. Can you feel it, Ms. Jensen?"

The ice surrounded them as they crawled to the dig site. Mary could see it soon enough, a few distant blips of black on the white horizon.

"There it is," he said, as they drew closer, the blips growing larger in their sight line. "Beautiful."

The site grew definition, and Mary saw it for what it was. A few temporary outbuildings surrounding a central drill, which rose twenty feet in the air. The dig team surrounded it, steam rising and the wind blowing it away in massive clouds. Schuller parked the tractor next to the other, and they got out. Mary bundled up against the hard cold. Still, it hit her like a brick wall. Schuller moved fast, ignoring the cold. She followed him into the largest outbuilding, adjacent to the hole and drill.

A heater occupied a third of the small room, with the science team and equipment filling all the other space. The three scientists studied a series of monitors, parsing through results from long strings of text.

"This is our home away from home," said Schuller. "As the team drills outside, we have multiple sensors pulling as much data as possible from the ice."

"What are you looking for?" asked Mary. "If they're invisible to the naked eye."

"With the nature of our science," said Schuller. "We are

watching for everything, basically. We have gotten to the point where we know something is down there. All preliminary readings have pointed to this place as the most likely. But that was our first challenge. How do you find something that has never been identified? Our answer was this. Every possible combination of sensors, testing for all known particles, collecting and gathering the statistics. If something anomalous appears, we'll know it, and our system will activate, trying to capture the data and the spark, as it were."

"How close are you?" asked Mary.

"Any day now," he said. "Hot water drilling isn't consistent, and certainly not out here. It could happen today, or in a week. But we are getting closer. We are fighting the weather, as every moment we're not working, the hole begins to shut, the environment trying to reclaim lost ground. So we must spend time each day reclaiming ground, so to speak."

"But nothing yet?" asked Mary, looking at the faces of each of three doctors, their eyes focused.

"No, not yet," he said. "But it will happen. I have never been more confident. The discovery is at our fingertips. We merely have to reach out and grab it. Would you like to see it?"

"See what?" she asked.

"The hole," he said, smiling.

Every time she went outside, the cold shocked her. The steam from the drill raised the ambient temperature outside a few degrees, enough to feel a difference. The roughnecks gathered around it, managing the pump, the drill, and all the other small settings that made the unwieldy machine churn through the ice, miles down.

Mike saw them, and turned off the drill. Steam rose from

the hole.

"Everyone does it once," he said, approaching them, pulling the layers of scarf off his face. "Take a look. I'm going to thaw inside for a few."

Mary walked up to the edge of the opening. A long cable held taut dangled below, the drill deep down at the bottom. The hole wasn't wide, only a few feet across, but Mary could follow down the strata of ice with her eyes. The interlaced spectrum of blues, whites, and grays traced back thousands of years. She followed it down into darkness.

"How far down is it?" asked Mary.

Beth uncovered her mouth. "Three and a half miles," she said. "We've made progress today."

"That's excellent news," said Schuller. "Excellent!"

Mary stood at the edge, staring down. Deep, deep down, where man had never been, never set foot, never even seen.

"We're drilling into a different time," said Mary, quietly. If anyone heard her, they didn't respond.

She heard a voice from behind her, but all that she could see was the hole, the layers of ice, the darkness covering everything. How far down could they drill, before they ran out of time to drill into? What was waiting down there for them? She imagined herself down at the bottom. Only the dark and million year old ice surrounding her. No light, nothing but the ice, and the dark.

The voice spoke again behind her.

Ice, cold, darkness, and eternity surrounded her. There was no escape. No humanity, nothing but the ice.

But that wasn't right. There was something else down there with her, something older than her, older than history. It was there, and it was there at the beginning, and then it was forgotten, sealed away, to be found much, much later.

A hand on her shoulder. Schuller's hand touched her shoulder. Soft at first, and then shaking. He raised his voice, for her to hear.

"Ms. Jensen," he said. "They need to get back to work. Would you like to return inside?"

She blinked and backed away from the hole, her dream dispersed. It already faded from her memory. She had been down in the ice—

with something, something else

They went back to the small outbuilding. That's where she remained for the rest of the day. The roughnecks hustled in and out. The scientists looked at the results and took short breaks, but never for long. They'd get back to work, poring over the data, looking for anything anomalous, double checking everything.

Doing this all day, out here on the ice. No wonder Helena stumbled, tired enough to slice open her own arm.

After a long day, they all drove back.

They reached the main camp, and Mary shrugged off her heavy gear, enjoying the steady, reliable warmth. Small conversations popped up between bites of food, but it remained silent otherwise. Bill made peach cobbler for dessert. He gave her a wink as he handed her a plate. It tasted great and felt even better, a reminder of the real world.

Something lingered in her mind. It held back some joy from her and robbed her of the pleasure of her favorite dessert.

Thoughts of the hole in the ice remained. She mentioned it to Jim, later on, and he said it did the same to everyone, no matter who you were. It caused strange thoughts. Nothing sinister, he said. Just the brain reacting to something it couldn't recognize.

She believed him, she did, but she was glad to be back in the main camp, away from the hole.

It felt wrong. Looking down into the ice.

5

Thoughts of the dig site lingered the next day. Helena had slept most of the previous day and wanted to go back out. Mary gave her permission, but warned her if she noticed any signs of fatigue she should stop immediately.

Helena left, along with most of the crew. Another day of drilling, staring at results, and waiting to hit depth lay ahead of them.

Mary went over their medical supplies, taking inventory. They had some painkillers, and the barest amount of surgical tools. If it came down to it, she could perform basic surgery. She had done it before. She had removed shrapnel from men, hoping to keep them alive long enough to get to a real hospital.

It was McMurdo if the weather was clear. And if it wasn't

clear—it was up to her.

With the lingering thoughts of the hole, the endless, depthless chasm, she felt doubt creep in. A tense gnawing anxiety in her stomach pulled at her insides.

Why did she come here in the first place? Her apartment in Chicago kept her safe and warm, Chinese takeout ten minutes away. So easily swayed. Mike had drawn her out onto the ice with one phone call. For all her skill and toughness, all it took was one call to drop everything.

Pft, there was nothing to drop.

She had no job, no friends to speak of. She had abandoned her past for Greg and then left him when the pain was too great. Even when he cried at her feet, she fled and cut him out of her life.

She had needed something new, and this was as good as any. If she wanted distance between the two, she had found it. Mike being the catalyst didn't hurt.

They had always worked well together, puzzle pieces that snapped to fit, right away. Even at the very beginning, her first contract after the service, the oil rig. She hadn't known what to expect. The rig pushed her to the edge. But she met Mike, and they became friends, and then lovers, and then partners. He carried her through it, and then she followed him, an easy package deal for recruiters. A seasoned medic, and an established crew chief. They got the job done. They could handle anything, especially together.

And then the contract would end. They would settle into an uneasy life, where neither knew what to do, looking for the next thing, always moving, never standing still.

And then she floated the idea of not moving. Of choosing a place and settling down. Of starting something. To get married, for a start. He agreed. It made sense.

And then Mike, steady and dependable, became erratic and flaky. She understood now. He had told her what she wanted to hear, and not what he wanted. Which was to flee. It came out eventually. They had a big argument, with neither backing down. It escalated into him declaring that he needed out.

And he left. But that was a long time ago. Worse things happened.

She woke up in the hospital bed. She was alone, machine beeping nearby, IVs running in and out of her. She traced them with her fingers; the plastic tubing foreign, sliding into her body. Where were they, where was Greg, the doctors, where was

And then Greg was there, holding her grasping hand.

"What happened?" she asked. "How is he?"

"You've had a hard night," he said, a nurse behind him. "We almost lost you. But you pulled through. James—didn't make it."

"No no no no no no no," she said. She squeezed his hand, and she heard him grunt in pain, and no James was a part of her, he was theirs, it wasn't this way, this wasn't it, this wasn't their future

Mike rapped on the door, and she was back.

"Hey doc," he said. "I need some help."

"Is that all you got?" she asked.

"It worked the first time," he said.

"I thought you were supposed to be out at the dig," she said.

"I tweaked my knee," he said. "Beth took the lead for the day. I can barely walk. I'd only slow them down out there."

"The bad one?" she asked.

"The very same," he said, limping into the room.

"Let me take a look at it," she said. "But I probably won't be able to do much."

"It's worth a shot," he said. "Maybe your magic touch will fix it right up."

"My magic touch hasn't worked in years," she said, rolling up his pants leg, pushing it up his thigh. "Where does it hurt?"

"Behind," he said. "Back of the knee. Any time I put weight on it, it kills me."

She touched it, fingers pressing into his flesh.

He winced. "Yeah, that's the spot."

"Tender to the touch," she said. "But can it support you?"

"Yeah, I think so," he said. "I worked on it the latter half of the day yesterday. Woke up with it screaming today."

"Then you probably just strained a tendon," she said. "If you tore it, not much I could do anyway, except send you back to the mainland."

"That's not an option," he said. "We've got work to do, money to make."

"I can give you something, a local injection," she said. "It should lower the swelling. I have a knee brace somewhere. If you stay off of it, and use the brace, it should make it possible. Some ibuprofen will help as well."

"Whatever it takes," he said. "Faster we get this job done, faster we all get home, and the faster we all get paid."

She grabbed the bottle, and drew a small syringe full.

"This will sting a bit," she said, and slid the needle into his knee, near the tendon. He didn't wince this time, and she pushed the plunger down.

"I'm sorry, Mary," he said, as she watched the syringe empty.

"Sorry for what?" she asked, only half listening.

"I'm sorry for leaving you when I did," he said. "How I did. It wasn't right. I know it doesn't fix everything, but I'm sorry."

She paused and pulled out the needle. "This is when you tell me? When I have a needle in you?"

"I just apologized for bad timing. I didn't say I've gotten any better," he said, half smiling.

She laughed, unable to help herself. His goddamn charm. Always got him out of messes.

"We haven't been alone," he said. "And I wasn't going to stalk you."

"So you busted up your knee to apologize," she said.

"You caught me," he said. "Guilty as charged. I purposefully stepped back wrong on it, after manhandling a thousand pound hot water drill into position, all the time thinking, this would be a great way to talk to Mary, and shirk work for a day."

"You're right, you haven't changed," she said, glancing at him, and then rummaged through the cabinets, looking for the thin sleeve that would cut down the swelling and help with flexibility.

"I am serious, though," he said. "I shouldn't have done that to you, no matter how I felt. It was childish."

She found it and turned back towards him, looking him in the eyes.

"It was a long time ago," she said. "Water under the bridge. I answered the phone, didn't I?"

"I meant what I said. I *am* glad you're here. I already feel safer."

"Didn't feel safe with the last guy?" she asked.

"Steve was good," he said. "But he's not you. He never saw combat. He didn't have experience on the rigs."

"Boot off," she said, and he pushed it off. She slid the sleeve over his sock, over his thick calf, and over his knee, firm around the joint. He winced again.

"Too tight?" she asked.

"Naw," he said. "Feels good." He swung his leg back and forth, and then hopped down off the bench, adding weight to the leg, until he stood on two feet again. He took a short walk, limping less than before.

"Stay off of it today," she said. "And see how you feel in the morning."

He sat down, sliding his boot on again.

"How you doing?" he asked. "Adjusting okay?"

"I'm alright," she said. "A little spooked by the visit to the hole, but otherwise I'm okay."

"It happens to everyone," he said. "It is not a normal thing."

"That's what Jim said," said Mary. "But it doesn't make the chill go away."

"Imagine how I feel," he said. "I'm the one making it deeper every day. I think it's because we can see down into it. Don't really do that for oil, especially out at sea. You're firing blind. Not here, not really."

"It gives me the willies," she said.

"You get used to it," he said. "As much as you can. It's just ice and some particles."

"The way Schuller talks about them," she said. "He makes it sound like they were delivered by God himself."

"He's getting high off his own supply," he said. "He wants what's down there to be so important, so *big*, he's talking it up to everyone, and he's done it so much, he believes it."

"Do you believe it?" she asked.

"I believe that we'll be getting a nice paycheck, and going back to civilization before winter rolls through. I get paid to make holes, not think."

She remembered Schuller's hands, steepled together as he talked over the particles, hidden deep in the ice. His erratic driving. The forged psych eval.

"You notice anything strange about Schuller's behavior?" she asked. "Anything worrying?"

He frowned, shook his head. "I know that looking at him, he seems kind of crazy, especially when talking about the mission, but he's the most steady one here. He doesn't get tired or lose focus, almost never raises his voice."

"Even when you're arguing with him?" she asked, raising her eyebrows.

"Not even then," he said. "He'll get frustrated, but considering the circumstances—he's as cool as a cucumber, as much as I hate it sometimes. Why do you ask? You testing us, doc?"

She looked at Mike's face, easy, full of charm.

"You keep this under your hat," she said. And she told him about the psych evals.

"Shit," he said. "Something's up with it."

"Oh, most definitely," she said. "But I have no real proof of anything. But when you talked about Steve's disappearance, and Schuller pushing people—seems like an awful coincidence."

"You're not wrong," he said. "But I just can't see Schuller

killing anyone. He's driven, and maybe even obsessed, but he almost always backs down in an argument. He doesn't like confrontation, or drama. And Steve and him got along great. Maybe the only person Schuller called by his first name, the only person he talked to about non-science stuff."

"But he's not upset," said Mary. "Hell, he called Steve selfish for killing himself out here."

"People grieve in weird ways," he said. "And I don't know. If I had someone I considered a friend kill themselves, I would be angry, doubly so when it was on the most important project of my life."

"Is it that big to him?" she asked.

"Have you heard him talk about it?" he asked. "He won't shut up. I'm glad he's out there in own little quarters, so I don't have to hear him lecture, on and on. And from what Jim has told us, this is his last shot at something real. If this doesn't pan out, he might not get funding for more field research. He'll have to go back to teaching, which he hates."

"And still none of it seems suspicious?" she asked.

"Does he seem like a killer to you?" he asked. "You've met some."

And she had. Met both enemies and allies who'd she'd give that title to, and Schuller didn't have the look in his eye.

"You don't hide something unless there's something to hide," she said.

"You're probably right," he said. "I'll watch him. But that's no different than usual. We all watch each other. It's the nature of the beast."

"Worse than the rig?" she asked.

"Way worse," he said. "The rig was dangerous, a living nightmare. But as long as there wasn't a storm coming through, you could take a walk outside. Shit, if it was sunny, you could even lay out for a bit. This might as well be Mars. You step outside the building, you have a damn good reason, and a little cabin fever just isn't good enough."

"I'm worried about everyone pushing too hard," she said. "It's how people die."

"We try and let off steam when we can," he said. "Jim invited you to the poker game, didn't he?"

"Yeah, but I'm terrible. He acted like a shark," she said.

"Pft, he's shit," said Mike. "He smiles like an idiot whenever he bluffs. You should play. We're all awful. It's right after chapel, in the big storeroom."

"Chapel?" she asked. "No one told me about church service."

"It's what we call Schuller's weekly meetings," he said. "It's tonight. You'll understand."

6

Mary had lost track of time in her office, doing research on hypothermia treatment. She arrived late to chapel.

Everyone else sat in two rows of folding chairs in the common room. Schuller stood next to the projection on the wall, displaying graphs and data.

"You can see we made good progress this week, and if we stay on this pace, we will hit target depth within the week—"

He paused as Mary sat down in the front row. She took the last seat, next to the science team. The roughnecks sat in the back row. Bill dozed, eyes half open.

"This is your first team meeting, so I will excuse your lateness, Ms. Jensen," he said. "But please try to be punctual from now on."

"Sorry," she said. "Won't be late for class again, professor.

Just had to get my books from my locker."

Schuller's brow furrowed at the muffled laughter from the back row.

"Yes," he said. "Just please be on time."

"I'll do my best," she said, a big smile on her face.

"As I was saying," he said. "If we continue at this rate of progress, we'll be hitting depth in a week's time, which is wonderful, and keeps us on schedule, ahead of looming winter."

He clicked, and the projector changed, a graph, with small print below.

"As you can see, the stream of neutrinos has not been interrupted since we started drilling, and in some cases have only increased, as I've shown before. Helena's work has proved time and again that all those signs point to this site as the correct one. On top of that, we have detected more and more high energy particles emerging as we get closer. There *is* something down there. And to think, they called this a fool's errand. We all will be laughing our way into the history books. They discounted errant cosmic rays coming out of the Earth—"

He laughed, and the scientists beside her chuckled. She had no idea what Schuller was talking about. Neutrinos? Cosmic rays?

He clicked again. Another graph, with a line sloping down.

"And now, sterile neutrinos have declined over time, as we dig deeper and deeper into the ice. That's actually a good sign, as super symmetry has always been theorized to be closely aligned to high energy particles—"

"Doctor?" asked Mary.

He stopped again, the laser pointer still pointing.

"Yes, Ms. Jensen?" he asked. "I've got two dozen slides to get through."

"This may be easy for you," she said. "But I don't know neutrinos from nacho cheese. Is there a way to explain this simpler? You told me about a divine spark. What does cosmic rays have to do with that? I thought they just gave people superpowers."

She heard another chuckle behind her, but Schuller remained nonplussed.

"I apologize, Ms. Jensen," he said. "This is your first team meeting, and I didn't go into proper depth in our debriefing. Let me explain."

He clicked twice, backing into the first slide. It showed the projected drill depth, the depth target, and other milestones.

"Last winter, various scientific outposts in the area detected cosmic rays emanating from within the Earth. And no, cosmic rays are literally just radiation from space. They were always that, before they were co-opted by Marvel Comics. And cosmic rays should not be firing outward, from Earth. They almost all originate from space."

"From here?" she asked.

"From Antarctica, in particular," he said. "From below us, in the ice. Miles below us, at the dig site."

"But how is that possible?" asked Mary.

"That's what everyone wanted to know," he said. "And there were several teams immediately trying to figure it out. The conclusion that most came to was a pocket of dark matter, somewhere in the Earth, that was releasing these cosmic rays. It was certainly a clean hypothetical, given the data we had, but all those other teams didn't have someone we did: Dr. Helena Darrow."

"Helena used the data from the cosmic ray's trajectory, and triangulated that with data we had from various high and low energy neutrinos. She built an algorithm that calculated the speeds and properties of all the particles involved. And after a lot of number crunching, it pointed to this spot right here. As the source of those cosmic rays. And it couldn't be dark matter, not in the ice."

"Then what is it? A spark?" she asked. Schuller's fingers moved again, becoming more and more energetic as he explained it.

"I was perhaps a little too poetic when explaining it, but frankly, it is not too far from the truth. Because after Helena's revelation about the location of the source, it brought an epiphany of my own, that if true, will shatter our notions of the origin of humanity. The age of the ice there is just over two hundred thousand years old."

He paused and let that number float in the air. Mary glanced down the row of scientists beside her, and some smiled, others nodded, while Andrew at the far end looked enraptured.

"Why is that important?" asked Mary.

"It is the same time as the birth of homo sapiens," said Schuller. "It is where we began our ascent, from picking through mud with simple tools to mastering technology and art. And I don't think that's coincidence. I *can't* believe it's a coincidence."

"So what's down there?" she asked. "What's the source?"

"It's not dark matter, but capable of producing cosmic rays. I believe it is a new elementary particle, one previously undiscovered, for whatever reason. I believe it is in some sort of stasis, down in the ice, trapped for us to discover. I believe that this particle is connected to us evolving into what we are today, responsible for our rise as the dominant life form on the planet. And I believe that when we find it, it will change not just how we view physics, but biology, sociology, everything. There will not be a human creation untouched by this discovery."

He got more and more animated, whipping the laser pointer back and forth through the air. Everyone paid attention now, even Bill behind her. The scientists sat on the edge of their seats.

"And everyone doubted us, doubted *me*. They thought the idea stupid, called it a waste of a good grant, waste of scientific talent, and told me that I would come crawling back to the academic life, my tail tucked between my legs. They told me that this was science fiction claptrap! Can you believe it?"

Schuller's fingers danced, his body moving back and forth in front of the projector as he spoke. The infographic became distorted as his body jerked in front of it. The image bounced around, painted on his figure as he moved, a shimmering portrait of belief.

"But we will have the last laugh. We will be vindicated. We will find what we're looking for, down in the ice, and we will return with a true discovery!"

His eyes gleamed in the projector's glow, his fingers moving even faster in the air, against his body, against the laser pointer.

Mary never went to church as a child. Her parents weren't religious. They believed in God, but they didn't believe in church.

"Buncha men taking my money, acting like they're giving it to God," her father said once, at the dinner table.
"Just stuffing it in their pockets. Who are they fooling? God
doesn't need money!"

But that didn't mean she had never gone to church.
Some of her friends went, and Mary would go along with
them on Sunday mornings. They'd stay up late the night
before, drinking soda, eating candy, and watching movies.
And on the Sunday morning after the sleepover, she went
with them, dressed in a white dress her mother sent with
her. She had been seven.

The church wasn't big, but big enough for seven-year-
old Mary. She sat with her friend and friend's family, and
older people said hello to her as they waited for the service
to begin.

It started and felt like many of the services she'd been to.
The pastor delivered a sermon and they sang songs. They
took an offering. She never understood her father, because
all the services she attended were nice. You didn't have to
give.

This church seemed a little different from the others.
They switched from sermon to music to testimonies and
back again. Men and women in the crowd would scream
to the sky and raise up their hands. They would fall down,
tumbling to the ground, before collecting themselves, being
helped up. And no one thought it was strange.

And then her friend fell, during a song. Not only fell,
but started speaking gibberish, a long string of noises coming from her. Her parents smiled. When she stopped, they
picked her up, crying tears of joy.

Mary didn't understand it. The believers surrounded her, and she realized she didn't belong here. She had intruded on them, and she couldn't understand their fanaticism. And looking at Schuller preach, and the faces of the scientists gathered there, she saw that same fanaticism, the same upward glance at Schuller as the men and women in that church had for their pastor. They worshiped.

"How do you know?" she asked.

It stopped Schuller, his fingers slowing down, his mania dissipating.

"Couldn't it be something else entirely?" she asked.

"No, you're right, Ms. Jensen," he said, smoothing out his shirt. "We can't count our chickens before they've hatched. But we're making history, either way."

He got back to his presentation, shuffling through slides detailing all the data they'd uncovered in the last week, going into incredible detail on every effort by every scientist, then allowing each to speak. Andrew went up first, one of the three scientists she met at the dig site.

Standing up, Andrew took awkward long strides to the front of the room. His delicate black hair fluttered lightly as he spoke. He seemed to have no patience for anyone but Schuller. Andrew talked about physics. Helena followed him to talk about more of the data. They delved further into subatomic particles, and Mary couldn't focus, no matter how hard she tried.

Jim went after both of them, talking about the ice samples they'd collected over the past week, and about the age of them, and the things they contained, and more data, small differences from previous ice that fascinated the science team, differences defined by measures too minute to see.

Jane spoke last. She studied geology, like Schuller. She had warm brown skin and looked winnowy and wispy, with close cropped black hair. After her time, Schuller came back up, and rounded off the presentation.

"All very promising material," he said. "I can't overstate my excitement. We are so close, and none of this would be possible without all of you. We are so so close, and soon, we will have the results we've been waiting and suffering for months for. Have a good night, and see you out on the ice tomorrow."

He dismissed us, and Mary helped Bill put the chairs away.

"What'd you think about that, Bill?" she asked, as everyone dispersed.

"The numbers don't do much for me," he said. "Over my head. But ole Schuller, he reminds me of this preacher my grandmomma would take me to, tent-pole revivals, out in the middle of nowhere in a field. He'd stomp, and shout, and everyone loved him. For a while."

"What changed?" she asked.

"They found out his side business, pimping out little girls," said Bill, putting up the last of the chairs.

"Jesus Christ," she said. "How horrible."

"Christ for sure," said Bill.

"What happened?" she asked.

"They strung him up from the highest tree," said Bill. "Put him up close to God. Right where he wanted to be."

7

Poker night was the first fun Mary had in Antarctica.

Mike, Bart, Beth, Jim, and her sat in the largest store-room, the largest card table they had set up in the middle, surrounded by cardboard boxes and wooden crates.

"Full house," said Jim, cackling, as he pulled his winnings in with two arms. His winnings consisted of a small pile of matches.

"You lucky bastard," said Mike.

"Better lucky than good," he said.

They had thousands of matches, an entire box worth, mis-ordered somewhere along the way, so they used them to bet. None of them had amassed a lot over the months.

They played Texas Hold 'em, and they passed being dealer around. All of them drank something. Jim and Mike both sipped on whiskey sours, while Beth had a beer. Bart just drank soda. Mary had a beer herself, but sipped it slowly, not wanting to get drunk.

"We all know you're not good," said Beth. "You don't need to be a doctor to see that."

They all laughed.

"Sorry, I didn't hear over how many matches I just won," he said. "I'm rich."

"Not a place on Earth they're more valuable," said Mary.

"Only problem is they'd never light outside," said Bart. "Too windy."

"My fortune," said Jim. "Blown away in the wind."

Play passed around.

"What brings you out here, Mary?" asked Jim. "Besides being friends with this asshole." He gestured at Mike.

"Hey," he said. "Birds of a feather flock together, dickhead."

"I needed a change of scenery," she said. "And then Mike called. Felt like the right time to push me out of my comfort zone."

"You couldn't ask for a place further from comfort," said Jim. "Next Mike here is going to drag you to outer space!"

"That might just be a bridge too far," she said.

"You served too?" asked Beth.

"Yeah, Marines. Afghanistan."

"My brother served there," said Bart.

"It was a shithole," said Mary.

"IED got him. Took his leg," said Bart. "He's lucky it was just his leg. I'm sure you saw worst."

"I was only in one firefight," she said. "I saw at least a soldier a week from the IEDs. Just brutal. Tying off arteries, telling soldiers their arms were gone. It was hard."

"This might be too much for me," said Jim, and he didn't look like he was lying.

"I'll change the subject. Three of a kind," Mary revealed three aces, and everyone groaned. She grabbed her matches and added them to her pile.

"You guys must be terrible, if you're losing to me," she said.

"You were sandbagging me," said Jim. "Playing me for a fool. You're a shark."

"When you're a minnow, everything looks like sharks," she said, smiling as she said it.

"Oh shit," said Mike, laughing.

"It's everyone pile on Jim day, I see," he said. "It's alright, I can take it. I'm the only man of science who will hang with you Neanderthals anyway."

"Yeah, what's with that?" asked Mary. "Why does everyone else hate us?"

"They don't hate you," said Jim. "They're just awkward people. Helena is perfectly nice, and probably would come if you ever asked her. I barely say a word to Jane myself, and we're basically in the same field. And Andrew—"

"Andrew is too busy licking Schuller's boots to do anything but," said Beth.

"I mean, I would have said kissing ass, but you're right," said Jim.

"And where's Teddy?" asked Mary. "Surprised he's not here."

"Teddy opts out of most team bonding exercises," said Mike.

"Why's that?" asked Mary.

"Because no one likes him, and he knows it," said Mike, smiling. "Don't get me wrong, he's a great worker, break his own back to help us out there, but in here, woo boy, he's sandpaper, all over."

"Speaking of kissing Schuller's ass," said Mary. "What the fuck is up with chapel?"

"Hey man," said Mike. "We wouldn't even be there if I had my way, but Schuller included mandatory team meetings in our contracts, including yours."

"I thought scientists were supposed to be rational," said Mary.

"When did I ever give you the idea that I'm rational?" asked Jim.

"I'm serious, Jim," she said. "That shit was creepy."

"I know, I know," said Jim. "It's his version of a pep rally. Being out here, alone on the ice, you know, can make you lose focus. He just wants everyone to realize what we're doing out here is important."

"I think he could do that without becoming a holy roller," said Mary.

"She's not wrong," said Bart.

"Listen," said Jim. "He's an academic, brilliant guy. Did some landmark studies just out of grad school. Put his name out there. That was fifteen years ago, and in those fifteen years, he's done nothing of note. Been laughed at behind his back. I should know, because I was one of those people laughing. And I don't think any of it is really his fault. Just had bad luck, time after time."

"Then why did you join up with him?" asked Mary. "If he's a laughingstock."

"One, there aren't a lot of glaciologist research positions

available," he said. "You should have heard my mom when I told her I was going to study ice for a living. She nearly died. Two, he's not wrong about the ramifications of this. If it bears out, if we find what we're looking for, it will change the world, change what we think about everything. It's not hyperbole. It *will* be groundbreaking. And three. Make fun of him all you want, call him a con man preacher, or whatever, but he is genuinely excited about what we're doing. Every single day he works longer or harder than all of us, and still maintains that genuine excitement about our work. And there's so little of that in science. I study ice because I find it exciting, and it's great to work for someone who shares that excitement."

"Anything to add to your monologue?" asked Mary.

"Yes," said Jim. "Straight flush." He laid out his cards and grabbed the matches.

"You son of a bitch," said Mike.

"So you've met my mother?" asked Jim, counting his matches and smiling.

The night wore on, and the piles of matches moved around. People drifted away, tired from the day. First Beth, then Bart, and finally Jim, tapping out when he went all in, and Mike called, taking all his matches.

Finally only Mike and Mary remained, playing hand after hand, barely paying attention to their cards. Mike had drunk five whiskey sours, and he slurred his words. His size had always obscured how drunk he actually was. Mary had switched to water after one beer.

"You buy everything Jim said about Schuller?" asked Mary.

"Jimsa good guy," said Mike. "And definitely not a liar.

Schuller gave him a job, gave him a purpose. Why would he dislike the guy?"

"I don't know," she said. "Does Schuller know you call it chapel?"

"I have no idea," said Mike. "I haven't told him, and he hasn't brought it up to me. Our discussions aren't always the most productive."

"Does he not respect you?" asked Mary.

"He respects me," said Mike. "He knows he'd be shit creek up without a paddle without us. Shit up creek."

"You're drunk," said Mary.

"I'm fine," said Mike, waving her off. "I think he just doesn't like the fact that we're not as invested in the dig as he is. We do what he says, we work hard, we're important, but we don't care like he does. And it bothers him."

"Let's get you to your bed," she said. "It's another long day out on the ice tomorrow. How's your knee doing?"

"It hurts like hell but it works fine," he said. "Which is all I need." He lumbered up, unsteady on his feet. Mary stacked the playing cards and tossed the empty beer cans into the trash bin. Mike folded up the card table, put it aside, and they left, turning off the light.

They should have called it quits earlier. The sun had set, and would be on a shorter clock everyday. Soon it would disappear for months, but they would be gone by then. They had stolen time, and they'd both be on short sleep tomorrow. It felt good to be alone together again. Mike would avoid a hangover, he always did. It never affected him like it did her.

He put her arm around her, and she helped steady him, even though he outweighed her by a hundred pounds. Everyone had shut their doors. She could hear the faint sounds of music from certain rooms, or someone watching TV on a tablet. She heard the wind howling outside, the winds getting worse and worse as the new season approached. They found his bedroom, at the far end of the bunks. Tucked under his arm, she could smell him again, the smell of his body, deodorant, shampoo, the detergent he used, even out here. It brought back those sense memories, of being curled up together on off days on the rig, throwing cash around when they got back home.

He leaned on the doorway.

Do you want to stay with me tonight?" he asked, looking at her, his arm still around her, his familiar strength right there.

She did. She wanted to, wanted to be with him, revert back to the version of her that had less accrued trauma, a ledger of pain that was limited to other people, and not herself. He was that. And she wanted sex. It had been a long time, and she could feel the pleasant anxiety burning inside.

"Not tonight," she said. "You're drunk. We're too old for this."

"You sure?" he asked. She could smell the booze on his breath.

"Yeah, I'm sure," she said. "Get some sleep, and I'll see you in the morning."

"Okay," he said. He half hugged her, and then leaned onto his bed. She closed the door, and walked back to her room, down the corridor.

She laid down in her cold bed. She felt tired, disappointed and proud of herself, for doing the right thing, but clearly not the thing she wanted. She wanted Mike, she wanted drunken sex, and she wanted her life before she lost James, pushed Greg away, and dropped off the Earth.

But Mike wasn't that, even if it would feel like it.

She laid down, and worried that insomnia would claim her, like it had in Chicago, night after night of sleepless drifting, pondering her mistakes.

And then she slept.

8

Mary forced herself out of bed the next day. She had hoped to have an easy one. Then Mike rushed back in from the dig site, carrying Andrew's unconscious body in his arms. He was pale, his lips and fingers blue.

The cold waited for you. If you weren't careful, just for a moment, it would make you pay. Weather in Chicago could be brutal, with temperatures dropping below zero degrees Fahrenheit. The rigs off the east coast of Canada were miserable in the winter, with frigid waters and howling winds.

They were nothing.

The cold in inland Antarctica is encompassing, unassailable. You can build bulwarks against it, like the buildings they lived and worked in, generators burning thousands of gallons of gas to heat them, to beat back the chill.

But it was always there. It would find your weak point and it would destroy it. The generator breaks, the furnace blows a fuse, someone forgets to wear one protective layer of clothing. It would come in and kill.

Someone stays out in the cold too long. Hypothermia sets in, and they shiver, a little at first, and then more, their whole body shaking, desperate for any way to generate warmth. Their heart rate, and their blood pressure rises. Their blood vessels constrict, with less and less blood reaching the skin, trying to preserve what little heat they have. It is defending itself against the cold. It is cutting off any unnecessary function, doings its best to stay alive as long as possible.

But it's a losing battle. The cold doesn't stop, not here. And the body can't hold forever. As its temperature drops even further, shivering becomes more and more violent, and the body's muscles stop behaving, stop listening to their master. The person slows, unable to process muscular movements. They become confused, their brain finally taking its toll from the cold. The skin gets colder and colder, and all extremities start turning blue, as the warmth in their blood retreats further and further inside.

It doesn't matter. The cold doesn't retreat and doesn't give up. The body continues to shut down all outer function as the cold invades. Heart rate, respiratory rate, and blood pressure all slow down, trying to maintain *something*. The brain suffers more, as the person's speech and motor functions struggle further. They'll begin to forget important facts, and their hands and feet become inoperable. All of their skin will turn blue, and they'll be incoherent. The cold continues. Frostbite will have set in by now, fingers, toes, lips, nose, and ears all suffering permanent damage, *if* the person survives.

At this point, they will take off their clothes, stripping off layer after layer of clothing, combative to anyone trying to stop them from further hurting themselves. At this point the surface blood vessels, having constricted to preserve warmth, cannot hold on any longer. They let go, releasing warmer blood back to the surface of the skin, which is now literally freezing. It burns, creating the illusion in the cold-addled mind of the victim they are burning up. So they shed their clothes, ripping off one of the few protections they have in this place. The cold persists.

This is the end. Their body temperature has dropped and dropped, now below eighty degrees Fahrenheit. It has shut down every single unnecessary function, and now major organs will fail. As the person dies, wherever they are, they'll burrow, digging into snow, or under furniture, to find a narrow, enclosed spot to die in. Their brain is in its most primitive state. The victim wants to hide, a last grasp at protecting itself. It is too late.

Andrew is still breathing as Mike drops him on the examination table, but his skin is cold to the touch, his lips and ears blue.

"What happened?" she asked.

"He stayed out too long," he said. "He was watching us work, making sure the sensors were arrayed correctly. And no one noticed something was wrong until he fell down."

"Christ," she said. "You're my temporary nurse. Grab the heating blanket, and get it on him." Mary grabbed a thermometer and pushed it into Andrew's ear. Seventy five Fahrenheit. *Jesus.* Mike came back, a thick blanket in his hands, built for extreme cold.

"Cover him, turn it all the way up," she said.

"Won't the heat shock him too much?" asked Mike.

"He can complain when he's conscious! Just do it," she said, readying an IV line, and grabbing a container of saline from storage. She handed it to Mike, with the heating blanket on full blast on Andrew.

"Put this in the microwave for two minutes, and bring it back here," she said.

"What? The microwave?" asked Mike.

"It's what we have," said Mary. "Go!"

Mike left, hustling out of the room. She pulled off Andrew's glove, trying to roll off his sleeve, and then just cut through the layers with scissors, revealing a vein. His thin arm felt cold. She tapped his arm and then slid the IV line in. She felt for a pulse.

She felt it there, barely. Andrew didn't move.

This was avoidable. This was avoidable.

Her anger rose, but she pushed it down. She needed to save him first.

Mike came back, holding the container of saline fluid between paper towels.

"It's hot," he said.

"It needs to be. It will cool fast," she said, attaching the bag to the IV pole, and then Andrew's line directly to it. The warm liquid flowed into Andrew.

"Now what?" he asked.

"Now we wait," she said. "And hope he wakes up. Why did he stay out so long?"

"I don't know," said Mike. "We were working our normal shifts, drilling, rotating people in and out of the outbuilding, but he stayed out. He was making sure all the sensors were hooked up correctly, aligned correctly. It's what Schuller told me."

"Where is Schuller?" asked Mary. If Andrew died, that'd be two deaths from the cold under his watch.

"Still out at the dig site," he said. "He told everyone to keep working while I brought him back."

Mary shook her head, her fingernails digging into her palms. She monitored Andrew's temperature as it rose steadily, the IV doing its job. But the temperature didn't tell the whole story. It wasn't an on/off switch. Some never woke up afterward, or some came back with brain damage, or lasting heart conditions. Or he could stay unconscious, in a coma, until his body finally gave out from the trauma. No one was meant to endure cold like this.

First up into the eighties, and then as he crested ninety, the true test was coming. She tested his pulse. It was stronger now, his lips and ears returning to their normal color. All good signs. And then his eyelids fluttered, fluttered, and opened, blinking, his eyes narrowed, darting.

"Where am I?" he asked. "What happened?"

"Back in the main camp," she said. "In medical. You were out in the cold too long. Mike, go warm up some chicken stock, in a mug. Bring a straw."

"I was just testing the sensors. I don't remember," he said.

"Don't talk," she said. "Just sit. You're still very cold. We're bringing your body temperature back up."

Mike returned with a steaming mug.

"Hold it up for him," said Mary. "Andrew, if you can, drink some of this through the straw. Slowly."

Andrew took the straw into his mouth and drank some,

taking small sips.

"I will look at your hands," she said. She pulled off his other glove, and the layers beneath it. She suspected there'd be frostbite, considering how long he'd been out. She examined his fingers, one by one. A few were blistered, with hardened skin, but they would eventually heal, perhaps with a lack of sensation, or with more sensitivity to the cold.

"I'm going to take your boots off now, and look at your feet and toes," she said. "How are you feeling?"

"It hurts," he said. "My skin is burning."

"It will hurt," she said. "But we need to know what you're feeling right now, before we can give you painkillers."

She pulled off his boots, untying sets of laces, and realized his socks were wet. *Oh no.* His feet got wet, maybe in run off from the drill, and he hadn't known it. She braced herself.

The color had returned to his feet. *But his toes, oh Christ, his toes.* He might keep a few of them, but most were too far gone, the skin blistered, turning blue-gray. She touched them with gloved hands. They hadn't warmed. Andrew couldn't feel her fingers. The tissue was dying.

She checked his temperature again, rising into the mid-nineties. His pulse had stabilized, and he seemed more alert. He held his mug as he drank.

"Andrew, I've got some bad news," she said. "Some of your toes have severe frostbite, and I don't know how many of them can be saved, long-term."

She expected crying, sadness, *something.* She had informed people of lost limbs and extremities before, and it had crushed them. They had lost a piece of themselves. Their body helped form their identity. They lost more than a finger, or an arm. They lost their *self*. It destroyed people.

Andrew's face betrayed none of that. "Anything else?" He sipped his cup of soup.

"It's hard to say," she said. "We'll have to monitor you, and see how your body reacts. Do you remember why you stayed out so long?"

"It's fuzzy," said Andrew. "But I know I needed to make sure the sensors were properly hooked up, and aligned. We were, yeah, we were getting weird data from an array, and they needed to be fixed. Dr. Schuller told me to make sure they were outputting correctly."

"And you never got a replacement?" she asked.

"I don't remember," he said. "I was trying to align the sensors, but it's hard with gloves on, and things started getting fuzzy, and then I was here."

Mary let Mike go, and then she held Andrew until his temperature reached normal parameters again. She bandaged his injured fingers and toes, to protect them. It would take weeks before the full damage was revealed. Until then, bandaging them was the only thing she could do, with a steady dose of painkillers.

"You need to rest," she said. "And stay out of the cold."

"I can't," he said, his face twisted now, distressed. "We're so close now. I need to help. I need to work."

"You nearly died, Andrew," she said. "Another minute or two, and you'd be gone. Your body has suffered severe trauma, and it needs to rest, and recover. At least two days, full rest, the bare minimum of activity. If these were normal circumstances, I'd be advising weeks, not days. So take your medicine and be glad you're alive."

She helped him to his room and then waited for everyone else to return from the dig site. Waited for Schuller. Mary found him in his lab, looking at some data.

"Hello, Ms. Jensen," he said, glancing at her, and then looking back down at his data. "I heard Andrew is doing well because of you. You've already proved your worth."

She beelined toward him.

"Are you trying to kill your team?" asked Mary. "Because you're doing a good job of it. One dead, and Andrew, nearly, today."

"What?" asked Schuller. "Of course not. It was a tragic accident—"

"You sent a man out into the cold, and didn't send a replacement, didn't check on him, for nearly an hour, when fifteen minutes is enough to kill!"

"I can't be responsible for everyone's well-being. Andrew knows the cold safety precautions. He's not a child," said Schuller.

"And then, *then*, when he's found unconscious, dying, you send him off, and keep everyone else there working?" asked Mary. "How can you be so heartless?"

"Me standing nearby will not decide Andrew's life or death," said Schuller. "We have work to do, and very little time to do it in—"

She grabbed him then, couldn't stop herself. Mary grabbed him by the lapels of his lab coat and shoved him back, into a nearby bookshelf.

"Ms. Jensen, I—"

"You have a decision to make," she said. "You have to decide what is more important, your team, or this mission. You can talk a big game in front of us every week, but when it comes down to it, you're not a leader. A leader *does* take care of every single person they're in charge of. A leader *does* treat their people like they are their children. A leader doesn't prioritize work over someone's wellbeing. Ever."

"It was an accident, Ms. Jensen, an accident," he said, stammering, looking away from her.

"What about Steve?" she asked. "Was that an accident?"

"He walked out in the middle of the night," he said. "How am I supposed—"

"And Andrew just stayed out in the cold a little too long," she said. "After a while, it's not a reflection on them. It's a reflection on *you*. And I won't abide it. Straighten up your ship." She let go of him then, backing off a step.

He straightened out his lab coat, still not meeting her eyes.

"I apologize, Ms. Jensen, please," he said. "I am under a lot of pressure right now. We are under a tight deadline, and I want to make sure we make it. We all do. I don't mean to overlook my team member's health. Andrew was the first I recruited, and he means the world to me. I promise it won't happen again. We're almost there."

"You will be without Andrew for two days," she said. "It should be more."

"We are understaffed already—"

"Two days, and you'll have him back. And he doesn't work outdoors at all. Understood?"

"Understood," he said.

She left him, her anger still simmering.

9

The days passed, and Schuller honored his word. He took more care. Andrew returned to work, even as the terrible damage to his toes was revealed. They got closer and closer to target depth.

Tensions had been running high, but it smoothed over as they had several productive, calm days in a row. Schuller even slowed down their pace as it became clear they would reach depth with time to spare. Even with the goal in sight, everyone dragged. The months of long hours wore on everyone, and Mary saw it clearly. They all became that much more irritable. The long hours plus the isolation equaled exhaustion.

Schuller practically danced his way to chapel. They would hit target depth tomorrow.

Everyone waited in their chairs while Schuller finished setup with the projector. There was something in the air. She could feel it. Excitement, anxiety? She had little invested in the research, but the scientists all buzzed. Even the roughnecks, normally slouched and uninterested, sat up and paid attention. Their work had gotten them this far.

"Hello everyone," he said, smiling. The projector showed the same slide from last chapel, but this time they were only a hair away from their objective. Schuller stood taller, his shoulders back, beaming like the Antarctic sun. He owned this moment.

"As you all know, we are close to target depth, and will easily hit it tomorrow. We've made steady progress, and despite setbacks and scares, we rolled on, kept our energy and effort levels high, and pushed through. And tomorrow, we'll have our results."

He clicked through slides, showing page after page of data again, all confirming their hypothesis. More high-energy particles, more reinforcements about the negative space. Still no more cosmic rays, but that was to be expected. Everything looked green for discovery.

The scientists went up, one at a time, and talked about their findings over the past week. Almost all their results pointed to there being something in the ice and in stasis. Andrew, still limping, went so far as to say that it's impossible there's nothing down there.

"Something is causing these results. And we'll find it tomorrow. Dr. Schuller?" he said, sitting down, as to not further injure his feet.

Schuller retook the slides and the focus, standing in front of them. He returned the slide to the first slide, showing them a slice away from discovery. He looked out at them.

"Today is the last day of this chapter of our lives. We turn the page tomorrow, start a new chapter, a new era. We stand on the precipice of greatness, and all we have to do is have the courage to step forward. Relish this night, because after it, nothing will be the same. For tomorrow, we will make a discovery that changes the course of human history. It will change how we look at biology, evolution, religion. This moment will be studied for years to come, and we are the ones here for it at ground zero. I've spoken before about the doubters, who've stood in our way, but tonight, I only want to focus on the positive, because frankly, those doubters will be forgotten. That will be history's judgment, while we will be remembered. Remembered for having the strength and fortitude to endure the cold, endure the isolation, and endure the hardship, to literally carve our way into the future. Because although we are unearthing something old, something *fundamental*, it is not the past we are affecting. This discovery will change the future of humanity, and *we* will all be here for it. And none of it would be possible without each and every one of you."

"Be emboldened by this. Be strengthened by this. Because it is a life-changing event, one that will incontrovertibly change the scope of all our lives. Be ready, because there is no going back. We tried to tell them that, but they didn't believe. But they will have to believe, after tomorrow. After we've shown them what we've discovered, they will have to move their rulers, and change their books, and permanently etch our discovery into the arc of human history. Every name here will be there, now and forever. So remember this moment, for the rest of your days. Remember this moment, and the one after, and the one after, because we will never ascend this high again. Despite that we are drilling deep down into the ice, we are ascending high, higher than humans have ever before. This is the end of the beginning. We will finally know our start, and with that knowledge, we can go further, go faster, and achieve more."

Andrew started clapping from his seat, and the science team followed suit. Mary clapped with them, and the roughnecks joined in. Mary understood Jim's statement about him. Schuller loved this, and it showed.

"Get some sleep tonight," he said. "For tomorrow, discovery awaits."

Schuller dismissed them, and Mary again helped put up chairs with Bill.

"Feeling especially motivated for tomorrow, Bill?" she asked.

"Absolutely emboldened," he said. "That's the word he used, right?"

She laughed. "Yeah, that was it."

"Well, Miss Mary," he said. "I'll definitely be emboldened when I make some scrambled eggs tomorrow morning. Most goddamned emboldened eggs you'll ever see. For the record books."

Everyone waited for her in the storeroom for poker night.

"Come back for more punishment, eh?" asked Jim, nursing a beer.

"No liquor tonight?" asked Mary.

"Last week's drinks did not sit too well," he said. "I think I'm beer only again until we get back to the mainland."

"Shouldn't be too much longer now," she said. "After tomorrow, right?"

"I imagine most of the science team will be staying until the last possible second," he said. "But not I. First opportunity for transport out, I'll be going. I miss my little girl."

"You didn't say you had a daughter," said Mary.

"You didn't ask," said Jim. "I should make it just in time for her birthday. I'm hoping I'll be able to bring her a small bit of Antarctic ice, from deep down."

"How old is she?" asked Mary.

"Seven," he said. "Perfect age. Old enough to have a brain, young enough to not have hormones."

"At least someone has their priorities straight," said Mary.

"Are you still holding a grudge against Dr. Schuller?" asked Jim.

"Andrew nearly died, Jim," said Mary.

"He seems fine now," said Jim. "Better than fine, actually. He's had more energy than me, and I don't have toes falling off."

"He did take it rather well," said Mary. "Which only worries me further."

"Andrew is a special case," said Jim.

"Special how?" asked Mary.

"He's the golden boy," said Jim. "Dr. Schuller's prodigal son. He's a genius. 23, graduated early, with a double doctorate, physics and chemistry. Did his thesis on Schuller's research work from back in the day. Idolizes him."

"Explains his fervor," said Mary. "But it won't fix his toes."

"Touché," said Jim.

"Accidents happen," said Mike, dealing cards, everyone settled. "You know that."

"Maybe you're right," she said. "Schuller gave a rather

impressive speech out there, even if a little blowhardy."

"Never heard that one before," said Bart.

"Look it up. Totally a word," she said.

"He's earned it," said Jim. "It's been a hard road here. He's been waiting for this moment a long, long time."

"I'm ready to get off this ice, and back to my warm bed," said Beth.

"Amen," said Bart.

"All our contracts have opt outs for the first ride back anyway," said Mike. "And a huge pay bonus if we stay longer than that. But I don't think we'll need to, thankfully."

"I'll take the warm weather," said Beth. "And Schuller can keep the extra grant money. It ain't worth it. I think I'll be passing on the next ice drilling contract, Mike."

"So will I," said Mike. "I won't freeze to death drilling for oil. Even on the oil sands."

"One more hard day," said Bart. "Woo boy, I am excited."

Jim shook his head. "About to make the scientific discovery of the century, and all you can talk about is going to bed."

"Hey man," said Bart. "I'm glad for you, I am, and Schuller can make all the pretty speeches he wants about the team, and effort, but our names aren't gonna be on any research papers, or in any record books. It'll be you guys. Which is fine. But like Beth said, my bed is the thing I'm looking forward to, not the discovery of the ages, or whatever Schuller said."

"Fair," said Jim. "Two pair, aces high."

"Oh fuck off," said Beth, throwing her cards down, two pair, king high.

"Thought you liked me, Beth," said Jim.

"I like you when you lose," she said.

"Just wait," he said. "You'll like me again."

Poker night zoomed by, with plenty of laughter to go around. No one drank much, just a little bit to loosen up. Mary and Mike remained to end the evening again. They put away the table and closed the storeroom.

Mike walked Mary back to her room.

"Thought I'd return the favor," he said.

"You're not carrying me," she said. "So it's not quite the same."

"Hey, I wasn't that bad," said Mike. "I was only a hair over the line."

"Alright, Stumbles," she said. "Whatever you say."

"I'm sorry," he said.

"I could get used to this apologizing," she said. "But I don't know what you're sorry for this time."

"For getting drunk, hitting on you," he said. "It was inappropriate."

"It's fine," she said. "Not a big deal."

"And thank you for turning me down," he said. "For being the responsible one."

"You're welcome," she said.

He paused, looking down, contemplating something.

"You alright?" she asked.

"What are we, Mary?" he asked.

"We're good friends," she said. "I think."

"Okay," he said. "That's good with me."

"If that changes, it can change on the mainland. Where we can think straight, and see the future," she said.

"That's reasonable," he said. He hugged her, and she returned it. It felt warm.

"Have a good night," he said. "Big day tomorrow."

"Wait a second," she said. He raised an eyebrow, stepping back into her room. "Andrew is still bothering me."

"What about him?" he asked. "He seems to be alright, at least as much as he can with what happened."

"That's what's bothering me," she said. "He almost died, is going to lose some toes, and he's fine. Happy to work next to Schuller. Schuller sent him out there to die, and he doesn't even care."

"You heard what Jim said. He idolizes Schuller. Golden boy, all that. You think a couple toes is going to change that?"

"It's not only Andrew," she said. "The rest of the scientists defending him. His speech tonight. It felt like he thinks he's a conquering hero."

"What else does he have?" asked Mike. "This is his whole life, and that was his last speech before everything starts falling apart again. The first departure date is a week away. There won't be any more chapel. He had to have his last sermon."

"It just feels like he's radicalized the science team. Even Jim," she said. "The way they look at him."

"They admire him," said Mike. "And that's okay. And soon enough we'll be gone, with thick wallets and heavy bank accounts. Don't worry about it. It'll all be over after tomorrow anyway."

"That's not true," she said. "Everyone is talking about tomorrow like it's a done deal. I'm not a scientist, but I do know that science is built on results. Not guesses. And all they've shown is guess after guess."

"They seem pretty confident," he said.

"That's what I'm worried about," she said, loud in a stage whisper. "Schuller most of all. He's so sure that they're finding exactly what he thinks they will. He's staked his reputation on it, his whole life even. And the scientists now are treating it like gospel. They haven't found anything yet."

"And?" asked Mike.

"What if," asked Mary, "They find something they don't want?"

10

They would hit target depth today, come hell or high water. Only Bill stayed behind at Tau.

The frigid cold couldn't dampen the excitement at the dig site. Schuller worked like a man possessed, double and triple checking equipment.

"We have to be prepared, have to be sure," he said. "We might only get one chance at this. Everything has to be aligned."

The drillers stayed focused, ready as always. Schuller gave them the go-ahead and they started drilling.

Everyone worked their normal routine, the drillers cycling in and out of the cold. Mary sat inside the outbuilding, watching it all happen. The wind blew hard and the dig team's breaks were getting longer and longer. Schuller eyed them, but said nothing. Mike could take criticism in a lot of ways, but if you interrupted him while he was working, he would blow up at you, and genuinely be scary. He didn't often use his size to intimidate, but he was proud of his work ethic. Question that and he wouldn't hold back.

The graphic displayed in chapel showed them a hair's breadth away from hitting target depth but in reality, hundreds of feet of uneven ice stood between the drill and the objective. It was slow going because it was always slow going.

The science team pored over the data, making sure they weren't missing a thing. They made clear that if the target depth was off, they would still be covered just in case their projections were off.

"I'm not getting readings over here," said Jim, his voice raising up over the din of the drill.

"I'll check the sensors," said Schuller, going outside himself.

"Stop, stop, let me fix something," he yelled, as he opened the door. Minutes passed, and the dig team came in, taking every opportunity to warm themselves, cramming themselves into the little outbuilding.

"How's it going out there?" asked Mary.

"It's brutal," said Mike. "The wind is just killing us."

"It knows we're getting close," said Teddy, his face covered by layers of scarves, two dark eyes staring out from within his hood.

Mary knew the weather wasn't getting more aggressive or trying to hold on to a guarded secret. But she wouldn't blame it if was. They were the aggressors here. Man wasn't supposed to be here, wasn't meant for this. Rising temperatures were the only reason the ice was open at all. They had carved desperate footholds in the frost, buildings here and there. After they left, the hole would vanish. Nature would reclaim the territory.

Several minutes passed. Just as Mike was about to pull Schuller in, he came in, panting, shaking from the cold, his eyelashes beginning to ice over.

"I had to replace the damn sensor," he said. "Mr. Hale, you can continue."

The drillers went back out, and the drill started chugging again as they drilled deeper and deeper, churning through ice as old as man.

But less than an hour later, the drill stopped. The engine quit. The roughnecks came back in, shaking off the cold.

"Engine died," said Mike. "Bart's looking at it, but it didn't look good. Be surprised if we can get it back and running today."

"What?" asked Schuller. "That's not an option. We were going to finish today. We're so close!"

"I can't *make* the drill work if it needs a part," said Mike.

"You can go retrieve it, and bring it back, and fix it," said Schuller, with certainty.

"After driving there, finding the part, coming back, it'd be a sixteen hour day," said Mike. "And that's if we don't face any more problems."

"This is the day, Mr. Hale," said Schuller, refusing to give up. "We've waited long enough—"

Bart came through the door, interrupting him.

"I can't get it to kick back on," said Bart. "Needs heavy work, probably multiple parts replaced. They're just burnt out."

"You heard the man," said Mike. He stood six inches taller than Schuller, and he straightened his back, showing his height. "We'll fix it tomorrow, and the day after we can hit the target depth."

"But—" said Schuller.

"Day after tomorrow, Doc," said Mike. "It's all we can do."

"Mr. Hale," Schuller said. "Please. Could you take another look at it, yourself? Just one more look. We're so close."

Schuller's eyes begged him. Mike gave in.

"I'll try," he said. "But no promises."

"Of course not," said Schuller, and Mike left, back out into the cold.

Everyone sat inside, the building starting to get warm from the stacked bodies. Minutes passed, and then the rumble of the drill started up.

"Amazing," said Schuller, and Mike returned, sending out the rest of the team to work while he warmed up.

"Thank you, Mr. Hale," said Schuller.

"It's running for now," said Mike. "But no telling how long it will last. Those parts will need to be replaced, sooner rather than later."

"I only ask that you do your best," said Schuller.

Time passed, and they got closer and closer.

The unpredictable ice wouldn't make it easy and the drill could die at any second. Schuller left the building, watching them drill outside, standing in the cold, just staring, unable to sit still inside. He would come in, check on the data, and then go back out, chill in his bones. Mary sat and watched it all, hoping it would be over soon. The tension affected even her. Schuller burst in.

"We've hit target depth," he said. "But we need a hundred more meters, to be on the safe side. We will hold our applause until then."

He went back out, leaving the building to silence. Everyone pushed hard, ready for it to be over, for the discovery to be found, unearthed, unburied.

Time crawled by out on the ice. Mary felt her heart racing, her hands trembling. She had no horse in this race and still, she could feel the anxiety. Her guts ached. Please, let them get there today. Please let this end. This can't go on any further.

She had been out there for a little over a week, and it felt endless already. The days stretched on and on, time pulled past its breaking point, where minutes and hours meant less and less, every single moment pushing, and she felt it now, sitting, waiting, hearing the wind hit the small building, their only protection from a cold death. She felt the distance, the infinite miles of ice and snow that stood between them and anyone, between life, between living. It had to end; it had to end.

The outer door creaked open, slammed shut, and the inner one opened. The harried face of Schuller appeared. He ripped off the scarf over his mouth.

"We hit it!" he screamed, and the science team roared in excitement. Everyone smiled, stood up and cheered. Even Jane was smiling, and Andrew picked up Schuller, shaking him in the air. Jim hugged her, and she hugged him back, happy for him. The anxiety building up in her vanished. It was over. They would have their results and everyone could go home. *She* could go home. No more cold. No more ice. No more worries.

"We hit it!" said Schuller, happier than she'd ever heard

him. "We got there! Everyone, examine the preliminaries. Andrew, follow me." He walked outside. Andrew followed behind him, as fast as his injured feet would allow. Mary bundled up and accompanied them. She passed the drillers as they came inside to thaw. Mike gave her a thumbs up as they passed. Everyone was happy.

Schuller stood in front of the drill, turned off.

"Do you have your phone?" asked Schuller. "Come on, hurry up, we need to get it now."

Andrew fumbled with it, but then held it out, recording Schuller.

"Go," said Andrew.

"We have just hit target depth, here at Research Station Tau, and have marked the greatest discovery of man in this century. As we study and dig into the results, I wanted to mark the occasion. First, I want to thank my science team. Doctors Barthes, Darrow, McTaggart, and Morroll have all worked hard, and this couldn't have been achieved without them. The drill team should be commended, who endured brutal cold as they drilled through the ice. Mr. Hale, Sizemore, Ramirez, and Ms. Simmons. I should also note our support staff. Mr. Norris—"

"Dr. Schuller," said Helena, her voice cutting through the wind, as she came stomping onto the ice, out of the outbuilding.

"Mr. Norris, Ms. Jensen, and I should also mention the recently passed Mr. Kennedy, a tragic accident that—"

"Dr. Schuller," said Helena. "There's a problem."

"I'm in the middle of this, Helena," he said. "Please—"

"You need to see this," she said.

"What is it?" he asked, excited, forgetting Andrew recording. Andrew continued, following their conversation. "It's as we expected, isn't it? What properties does it have? Did we capture it? We captured it, didn't we. They won't believe it. Oh, I'll make them eat their words—"

"Doctor," said Helena. "There's nothing."

"What?" asked Schuller. "That's impossible."

"I looked at everything, all the results, from the moment we cracked the depth, to when we turned off the drill."

Schuller's face had fallen, horror overtaken it from the happiness he just had.

"No results. Nothing strange. Nothing out of the ordinary. Nothing."

11

"Impossible," said Schuller. "Double check everything. Even preliminary results should point to something."

He rushed back in, Andrew scrambling after him. The anxiety in Mary's gut returned, lingering again.

Everyone had crowded inside, and the raucous laughter and joy that filled the small room when she left had vanished. The place had gone silent. The roughnecks stood to the side, looking at each other. She caught Mike's eye, raising her eyebrows. He raised his in return.

"It's impossible," said Schuller, repeating himself. "Hand check everything. The computer could have easily missed something, dismissed a result that's important."

The science team pored over the results, as everyone waited. Mary began to sweat under her parka.

"Still nothing," said Helena.

"I don't believe it," he said. "I won't believe it. Look again. Cross check the sensors; see if they have any similar holes."

"I can't," said Helena. "Not out here. I need the computers at base. Not enough processing power. It would take days."

Schuller's eyes darted to her with venom, but he said nothing. Instead, he went to Mike.

"Mr. Hale," he said. "I need you to continue drilling. Another hundred meters. We may not have dug deep enough."

"We went well past the estimated target depth," said Andrew, his voice low.

"Don't question me," said Schuller, angry now.

Mike looked at him, shrugged, and went outside. The dig team trailed him.

"Jim," he said. "Go examine the sensors. Make sure they're properly aligned and functional. I swear, if a broken sensor cost us the find of the century."

Jim bundled up and left, without glancing at Schuller.

"ANITA would pick up something," said Helena. "Even if our sensors missed it."

"I will not let NASA have our glory," said Schuller. "We worked ourselves to the bone for this, and we will get the credit we deserve."

"I'm sure it's something simple," said Andrew. "That we missed. We'll find it. We just have to collect ourselves."

Mike came back in. The sound of the drill kicking on never happened.

"Well?" asked Schuller.

"It's done," said Mike. "It needs repairs, and we don't have the parts here. We can work on it tomorrow, get it up and running. But it'll take at least a day of work. Pushing it further today blew another part."

"That is—is unacceptable," said Schuller. "Make it work."

"Doctor," said Mike. "I am not a magician, and unless you are, that drill will not be working again today. Feel free to look at it all you want, but my team is returning to base. We are tired and cold, and tomorrow will be another long day."

"You can't just leave," said Schuller, indignant. "It's still down there, I know it."

"We're heading back to base," said Mike. "And I'd advise you to do the same. You're not thinking straight, and it's going to hurt your work."

"He's right, Dr. Schuller," said Andrew. "We should go back, and take a longer look at the results. I'm sure it's hiding right underneath our noses, I'm sure of it. With the better computers, more time, and some rest, we'll see it quickly."

Schuller's shoulders loosened, and his face softened. He looked at Andrew.

"You're right," he said. "You're right. Science isn't done in a day. Let's head back to camp, and we can examine the data more closely. I'm sure we'll find something."

They closed down the dig site. Everyone returned to base to rest and eat. Mary checked on both Helena's arm, which was healing, and Andrew's toes, which were showing further and further signs of decay, turning darker and darker by the day.

"It looks like you'll lose seven toes," she said, as he slipped his socks back on, and then protective boots. He didn't answer her.

"Andrew, did you hear me?" she asked. "Are you alright?"

"I know you think it's weird that I haven't reacted more,"

he said.

"I'm worried about you," she said. "Sometimes delaying emotional acceptance of lost extremities can cause problems down the road."

"They're just toes," said Andrew. "Frankly, it's not that much to give up, considering what Dr. Schuller has done for me. I would sacrifice more for this discovery. To be a part of this."

He left. By the time she went to sleep that night, the science team still worked, analyzing the data with the aid of the more advanced computers at the main base.

The next day the dig team left to repair the drill, just six days before the opt out date. The scientists kept their head down, digging through the results. Mary felt the tension in the camp.

Mary sat alone in the mess hall, the science team all eating at their desks. Bill ate with her.

"Feelin' kinda spooky in here," said Bill, drinking a coffee with his pulled pork and macaroni and cheese. "Any word if they've found anything?"

"I haven't heard anything," she said. "Preliminary reports were nothing."

"That's a hard pill to take, after all this," he said. "You taking the opt-out date in your contract?"

Mary hadn't thought about it. If she left, anyone remaining would be on their own in any kind of medical emergency.

"I don't know," she said. "I don't want to abandon anyone."

"I mean, it's on the dotted line," he said. "I, for one, don't see any point in sticking around. I'm just a butler, anyway.

They don't need me. And believe me, Miss Mary, you don't want to be here in the winter. You get out while you can and call that a win."

"I don't think Schuller will call anything beneath his highest expectations a victory," she said. "He was angry yesterday. Practically snarling."

"How'd you grow up?" he asked.

"What do you mean?"

"Were you poor? Middle class?" he said. "Don't imagine no rich kid's gonna go be a Marine."

"My dad was in the Marines," she said. "Was an officer, eventually. But we never had a lot of money. Enough to get by."

"We were poor," he said. "Had to scratch through the dirt to get a penny. Sometimes dinner was just going to bed with an empty stomach."

"Sorry to hear that," she said.

"Ain't nothing," he said. "I've gone way farther than my daddy ever did. I'm on the edge of the world. He never even left Georgia. And sometimes early losses help make the later ones not so bad. That's what Schuller don't understand. Won't never understand. He's never gone to bed hungry. Never struggled with just living. He thinks losing this is all there is. It ain't good."

"Maybe they'll find something in their results," she said.

"I doubt it," he said. He ate some macaroni.

"Why do you say that?" she asked.

"All that talking that Schuller did," said Bill. "All that talking was about how momentous this will be. How important it is. And how hyped he was they was going to find it yesterday. He didn't act like it'd be hard. For him and the science types, it'd be plain as day. But they're digging for something now. Needles in haystacks. And my thought is they already did the digging, out there, on the ice. They didn't think they'd be doing it twice."

"I hope they find something," she said.

"I hope they do too," he said. "But I'm not holding my breath. And I've already started packing. My momma's biscuits are waiting for me."

"Sounds good," she said. "Is she as good a cook as you?"

"Better," he said. "You swing on by momma's house, and you can have some biscuits too."

"I just might," she said.

*

Bill was right. They had no good news.

The dig team came back looking rough and tired. They had wrangled equipment all day, in the cold, and the drill wasn't fixed. It would take another day.

"But you said it'd be working today," said Schuller. Their voices carried through the entire building. Everyone could hear them.

"I was wrong," he said. "There were more problems than we thought. The systems don't work the same in the cold. I thought once we replaced the parts, it would start. But the whole system needs new oil and lube, and we're going to have to lather it on thick, to each and every moving part. We can do that tomorrow, and then it'll be up and running."

"You said that yesterday," said Schuller.

"I told you, I was wrong," said Mike. "I have no problem admitting it, when I know it."

"What are you implying?" asked Schuller.

"Did you get any results today, Doctor?" asked Mike.

"No," said Schuller. "Nothing. But we'll continue looking. It's hiding in the data, somewhere. And we'll keep digging. We'll find it. We have to keep trying."

"Our opt out date is in five days," said Mike. "And the entire dig team is taking it."

"You can't leave," said Schuller. "We need you more than ever. Just a little further, Mr. Hale."

"I'll fix the drill," said Mike. "And we'll work until the departure date. But no further. It's not worth staying."

"I see it now," said Schuller. "I see everything. And I assume the drill will still need more work tomorrow, and the next day, and the next day, until the day to leave comes, and then voilà, no more digging."

"Excuse me?" asked Mike.

"You've been slacking this entire time," said Schuller, almost yelling now. "Taking longer and longer breaks. Delaying the dig. And now, when we are faced with a setback, you cut and run."

"You question me or my team's work ever again, and you'll have much larger problems than not getting the results you wanted," said Mike, his voice booming. Mary got up from her desk, walking down the hall. The argument continued, both yelling now.

"Oh, the brute threatens me," said Schuller. "All your strength can't hurt me anymore, Mr. Hale. What more could you do to me that the academics haven't?"

"Do you want to find out?" asked Mike, and Mary got between them, pushing Mike back. She could feel the tightness in the muscles in his chest.

"What I want is for you to show some backbone, and stay, and help us," said Schuller. "We are still so close, and all you are doing is leaving. All we need is another push, another hundred, two hundred meters, and we'll find what we're looking for."

"Is that what you're telling your team?" asked Mike, as Mary backed him up to the door. "Are you telling them we're almost there, we're almost there? Keep working one hundred hour weeks. Keep pushing with little or no sleep. You'll find it, you'll find the discovery, which will have my name on it, front and center. You've used the words almost there a thousand times, Doctor, and I've gotten sick of it. Well guess what, it's almost time for us to go home, and finally get off this hellhole!"

Mike's body shook with every word. She had never seen him let loose like this. He had held it back for months, but Schuller had pulled it free. They would not rebuild.

"There's nothing out there, Doctor," he yelled, as she backed him out of the door and down the hall. "There's nothing out there, and this was all a waste of time and money. You failed, Doc, you failed. There's nothing out there!"

12

Bart was the first to report hallucinations.

She didn't know much about him and hadn't spoken to him outside of the poker games and a few interactions in the mess hall. He was young, in his early twenties. A big brawny kid that Mike had taken a shine to in the oil sands. He didn't talk much, but laughed a lot, and followed Mike around like a lost puppy dog. Mike had mentored Bart, so he could run his own crew one day.

They had started digging again, the drill running smooth. Only Schuller and Andrew went to the dig site with the roughnecks, hoping desperately their initial depth estimate was wrong. Three days remained until the opt out date. They had scheduled the helicopter.

He knocked on her office door, three small raps. Bart

stood there, looking away, down the hall.

"Bart," she said. "What's up? Everything go okay today?"

After their big fight, Schuller had apologized to Mike. Schuller needed him and Mike wouldn't have backed down. He didn't lie when he said he would admit when he was wrong. If he thought he was right, he'd never back down. It didn't ease the tension, with the other scientists cross checking all the results, verifying everything they could. They had found nothing.

"As well as it could," he said. "No injuries. No results, either. We went another couple hundred meters down. Still nothing."

"So what can I do?" she asked.

"Can you give me a physical or something?" he asked, not making eye contact.

"Why? You alright?" she asked, standing up.

"I've just felt funny lately," he said. "I can't really explain it. Was hoping you could do tests or something, make sure I'm alright."

"I can do that," she said. "Come in, close the door."

"Sit down," she said, and he sat down on the exam table.

She looked at his eyes, ears, mouth. She listened to his heart and took his blood pressure.

"Blood pressure is a little low," she said. "But it's probably because you haven't eaten dinner yet. No worries there. Nothing wrong with your sinuses, eyes, or ears. Temperature is normal, if a little low. Lay down."

He laid down, and she listened to his abdomen, putting pressure on the typical spots.

"Any discomfort?" she asked.

"No," he said.

"Sit up," she said. She tested his reflexes, elbows and knees.

"Your reflexes are a little slow," she said. "But again, the cold, working all day, not eating. There's nothing physically wrong with you, as far as I can tell. The next step would be a blood and urine test, but we don't have the capabilities here. McMurdo has a lab, but that might as well be on Jupiter at the moment."

"Well, thanks for trying," he said. "At least nothing's wrong."

"When you say you felt funny," she said. "What do you mean? Can you be more specific?"

He hesitated, opened his mouth, and closed it.

"Bart," she said. "If something's wrong, tell me."

He looked at her, in the eyes, the first time since he walked in the door. She saw the fear in them.

"I've been seeing things," he said.

"Things like what?" she asked.

"Weird stuff," he said. "Stuff I can't explain. Like, I'll be looking at Mike, or Beth, talking to 'em, and I blink, and it's not them anymore. It's something else."

He still held something back. "What something?"

"I can't describe it, because I never seen anything like it. It was a monster. Kind of like a bug. Big eyes, weird mouth, and like, hard skin. Scaly, a dark blackish green. Antennae."

"Mike and Beth looked like monsters?" asked Mary.

"Not just them," he said. "Everyone."

"Even me?" she asked. "Right now?"

"No," he said. "Not right now. It happens fast. I'll be having a normal conversation, or just sitting, eating, listening, watching. And then they switch, between blinks, whenever my eyes are closed. I open them, and boom, monsters, all of a sudden."

"How fast until they switch back?" she asked.

"It changes," he said. "Sometimes it's like a light switch, on and off, I blink, they're gone, and then, I blink, they're back. Other times, it's for entire conversations. And sometimes—"

He stopped, hesitating again. She pushed him.

"Sometimes what?" she asked, worry building inside her.

"Sometimes it doesn't turn off," he said. "Sometimes, it just stays. I can't look at Bill anymore, because he's not Bill anymore. He's a monster, now, and has been for the past day."

"Bart—"

"I know it's not real," he said. "I know I'm seeing things. People talk about it, cabin fever, whatever. I've never had a problem with it before, and at first, I thought it would go away. It hasn't, so I wanted to talk to you."

"It was the right thing," she said. She'd never heard of cabin fever making people see bug monsters, but at least he came to her. When someone out on their own starts seeing things—it's when things can get dangerous.

"When did it start?" she asked.

"It started with dreams," he said, answering a different question. "Really vivid dreams. I never remember my dreams, or my nightmares. But these, I remembered everything when I woke up."

"What were they about?" she asked.

"I was with my family, back home, in Iowa. On my grandpa's farm. It wasn't a big farm, I know that, but still, it was a healthy chunk of land, before he got squeezed out. But it looked so small in my dream. I was standing on his porch, looking out onto his land, and it looked tiny. The crops, the animals. He had a milk cow, that I named Dave. She was beautiful, so sweet, and Dave was there, but small, just like everything else. And I stepped off the porch, to look, and when I looked back, the house was small too. And it wasn't that I felt big. Everything else just felt real small. And then my family was on the porch, all of them, even grandpa, who's been dead for twelve years. They were all looking at me, and even though they were so small, I could see their faces. And I knew they hated me. I could feel it, you know? I could just feel their hatred for me, like this dark feeling, coming at me, in waves. And then I knew that the me in the dream didn't love those people. You know, like I'm looking at my family, all together, and I felt nothing about them. They hated me, but I didn't hate them back. I just felt nothing towards them."

"That sounds more like a nightmare," she said.

"What?" he asked, like coming out of a daze.

"You said it started with dreams," she said. "Not nightmares."

"Yeah," he said. "I guess you're right."

"How long between the nightmares and the hallucinations?" she asked.

He blinked. "Um, maybe a day."

"Okay," she said. "I don't want you working anymore. Rest, take it easy. It probably is just stress induced, with the isolation. It might just stop once you relax, once we get out of here. Once we get back to McMurdo, the people there can look at you, and we'll take it from there, get you back to the mainland if that's what it takes. Until then, no working, and if it gets worse, you immediately come to me. Don't stop, don't pass go, immediately come to me. Understand?"

"I understand," he said. "There was more, though."

"More what?" she asked. "More nightmares? More hallucinations?"

"Well, yeah, I could describe more, if you wanted, but that's not what I was talking about," he said. "It's the thing I was talking about first. The funny feeling."

"The hallucinations weren't enough?" she asked. If she started seeing things, she'd sure as hell tell someone.

"They messed me up, for sure," he said. "But I still knew they were wrong, right? Like, I knew that I saw Mike, and then he turned into a monster, that he was still Mike, under there. Mike's not a monster. I knew I was seeing something wrong, something that didn't belong. But the new thing—I-I don't know what it is. I was hoping you'd find something in me that could explain it."

"Explain what?"

"I've felt—" he said, struggling with his words. "I've felt not alone."

"Can you explain?" she asked.

"I'm trying," he said. "But it's hard. I've never felt anything like it before. Well, maybe that's not true. Maybe, maybe there was one time?"

"When was that?" she asked.

"It's when I got baptized," he said. "I was little, like five or six, and I was getting baptized. So I was in front of the whole church, all my family, and all the folks from town. I'd been around these people my whole life, they all knew me by name. John from the grocery store in town, Lana from the feed store, old Esther, who played organ—"

"I get it," she said.

"So the pastor is there, and me, and we're standing in the water, in these white robes. And I was a little kid, so I was nervous. I didn't know what to do really, and I was in front of so many people, really for the first time. But then, he dunks me, real gentle, and then I come up, soaking wet. The pastor is talking, and the whole crowd is cheering me, applauding, my older cousin Jenny even whooped, and I felt kinda the same feeling."

"So it was a good feeling?" she asked.

"No," said Bart, immediately. "No, it felt horrible."

"I don't understand," she said.

"When I'm with friends, or family," he said. "It feels good. But it's not the same as that feeling. I'm still me when I'm with them. I'm not alone when I'm with them, but I'm still alone inside."

"I'm confused," she said. "Is there another way to explain it?"

"I'm sorry, I'm trying," he said. "It's weird, and I'm not great with words-"

"It's alright," she said. "Just do your best."

"Alright, so I felt like I wasn't alone inside," he said, pointing at himself, at his chest. "Like there was something there, something else, *inside* of me, *with* me. Like, oh, I got it. Imagine there's a bucket, filled with water. And the bucket is my body, and the water is me. All of it. Everything I do and think, right? And imagine there's a cup, like a big gulp maybe, and it has another liquid, like Mountain Dew. It feels like someone poured that cup into the bucket, and some of me sloshed out, and now that bucket has both the water, and the Mountain Dew, mixed together. Not alone anymore."

He looked at her, and his fear had risen to the surface again. Explained why a cord-fed country boy who probably hated doctors came to see her. Nothing in him could explain it.

"Does it still feel like that?" she asked.

"Not right now," he said. "It comes and goes."

"Well, if you feel like that, you come get me. I don't care when it is, or what I'm doing, you stop me, and you tell me. Understand?"

"I understand," he said. He started getting up. She went to her desk. She needed to write all this down, and send a message to McMurdo. They needed to know.

"They'll fix me, right, Mary?" he asked, his hand on the doorknob. "At McMurdo? Or on the mainland?"

"Yeah, they'll fix you," she said. "It'll be okay."

He smiled, lopsided. "Good," he said. "Because if I had to keep living like this, I couldn't. I wouldn't be able to take it."

"Bart," she said. "When was the first nightmare?"

He counted on his fingers. "Three nights ago."

"Rest," she said.

"Will do," he said, and he left.

Mary pulled Bart's psyche eval, looked it over. Nothing strange. No history of mental illness or stress-induced issues. Solid as a rock, which matched her eye test. He was a good kid who didn't cause problems.

She finished her report, including all the dates he had given her, when she saw it. How could she not have seen it faster?

His first nightmare was three nights ago.

The first night after they hit target depth.

13

She found Mike that night to tell him.

"You're telling me that I look like a bug monster to Bart?" asked Mike, sitting on his bunk. They were alone in his room. She didn't want anyone else knowing, not yet.

"Sometimes," she said. "We all do."

"Bart's just about the most level-headed dude I've ever met," said Mike. "That's why I like him. And it hasn't been *that* long."

"You know there's no hard and fast rule," she said. "Isolation affects people different ways, and sometimes doesn't affect the same person the same way at a different time."

"But still," he said. "He'd be the last guy I'd guess would get the willies."

"He did the right thing," she said. "He came to me, told

me what was happening. I told him to rest, to report any other hallucinations."

"Have you told anyone else?" he asked.

"Not yet," she said.

"Good," he said. "Don't tell anyone. Especially Schuller."

I don't like him," she said. "But he's the lead on the station. He should know if someone is suffering from delusions and hallucinations."

"It's tense enough around here as it is, without everyone worrying about Bart. Bart's not a problem. I know him, trust him. Schuller is the problem. He's getting worse every day."

"Schuller isn't having hallucinations," said Mary.

"No, but his obsession is getting worse."

"What if he asks why Bart isn't going out on the ice?" asked Mary. "He'll want to know why you're down a man."

"Tell him he's sick," said Mike. "Tell him he had a panic attack. Just don't tell him about the hallucinations. And for sure don't tell him the story about Bart and his bucket. We'll be gone in three days, and none of it will matter. But I don't want to give him any excuse to pick a fight. We can manage with three. Teddy and Beth will understand. I'll make them understand."

"I'll cover," she said. "But if he gets worse, I won't be able to hide it."

"Fair enough," he said. "We'll have different problems then."

Mary felt exhausted. They all did. She retreated to the solace of her bed.

She was pregnant again.

She blinked. She sat at their dining room table, her laptop open. The screen showed a Pinterest board full of baby room ideas. Greg wanted blue or pink, a traditional color, regardless of gender. She wanted a neutral color or to paint a mural. Her friend Adam painted and said he'd do the room for free as long as he could put the finished project on his Instagram.

"Are you ready?"

She looked up. It was Greg, dressed and ready to go.

"Yeah," she said. "Just killing time."

"I'm nervous too," he said, rubbing her back. "We should go if we want to make it on time."

He drove, her in the passenger seat. They would see their baby for the first time. All of her friends with kids told her it was an amazing experience, a chance to see the child growing inside of you, but she only felt anxiety. What if something was wrong with them?

Her parents had always warned her, always told her that when she had her own, she would understand the desperate need to care for her child, like they had cared for her. But her mother never warned her about the terror or anxiety of caring about something this much. She had done everything right. She changed her diet, hadn't touched a drink, exercised some, but not too much. She read every parenting book on the planet, stacks and stacks of baby books, many of which were hand-me-downs from her friends with older children. None of them described the fear, certainly not to the depth she felt.

"Tell me everything will be alright," she said, looking out the window. Greg drove, one hand on the steering wheel, the other holding hers. He didn't complain, her hand sweating all over him.

"Everything will be alright," he said. "We'll find out we

have a healthy boy or girl, and we'll get to see them for the first time. It's normal to be worried."

They got to the doctor's office, and her anxiety multiplied. She felt dizzy as she walked in. Her chest tightened.

They checked in. The fear inside her simmered. She forced breath in and out, trying to push some of the fear away. It didn't work.

A pregnant woman walked out through the waiting room. She held hands with her husband, and the couple exchanged a glance between them, one of love. The pregnant woman looked at Mary, smiling at her, a smile of a shared predicament, of encouragement. Some of the fear disappeared. It *would* be okay. She felt the baby inside, and it would be okay.

"The doctor will see you now," a nurse said, walking up to them. They followed her, down some winding, antiseptic hallways. They went into a room with a big screen on a moving display and a large padded seat dominating the middle of the space.

"Mrs. Hoffman," she said. "You can sit there. I'll be right back with Dr. Stevenson."

They were in the room now, and more of her anxiety vanished away. It wasn't so bad now that they were here. It wasn't all gone, but it was tolerable. A normal amount, an amount that she could live through.

Dr. Stevenson arrived in a few minutes, smiling, calm.

"Mary, Greg," he said. "Nice to see you. Mary, how are you feeling?"

"Worried," she said. She never lied to doctors. She never wanted her own patients to lie to her.

"Perfectly natural," he said. "But everything will be okay.

We're going to find out if your baby is a boy or a girl, and determine their health. You're both in great shape, with no family history of birth defects. I don't foresee any problems. Are you ready to begin?"

Mary pulled up her shirt, revealing her growing belly.

"This will be cold," he said. He squirted some gel into his gloved hand and then rubbed it on her stomach.

"Whoo," she said. It was cold, bracing. He rubbed it all over and then turned on the screen, the ultrasound paddle which would see inside her and give them a picture of their baby.

"Let's take a look," he said, and began passing the paddle over her stomach, gliding over the gel and her skin. It created a picture on the screen, building an early portrait of the baby. Minutes passed. The portrait grew as the ultrasound waves passed through her.

Greg sat next to her, holding her hand. She studied the screen, seeing the image of her baby. She couldn't make it out, but she saw rough shapes, cylinders and spheres. Were those fingers? She couldn't tell.

He stopped.

"Well, that's unfortunate," he said.

"What?" asked Mary. "What's wrong?"

"You can see it, as clear as day," he said. "Didn't think it was very likely in you two, but I was wrong. It's a pity. Do you see it, Greg?"

He sighed next to her. "I do," he said. He still held her hand.

"What?" she asked. "Someone tell me what's going on!"

"It's not human," said Dr. Stevenson, his face grim. "You can see the ancillary limbs, the stalks right there. That's one, two, three, four, five eyes. I'm sorry, Mary, I really am."

She looked at the picture, and it looked like a human baby. It looked normal.

"What, no," she said. "It's my baby, it's normal."

"I'm sorry," he said, standing up. "It's really not. And we have strict guidelines in place. Nurse?"

The nurse was there, handing him a scalpel, and then moved next to Mary.

"Hold her down, please," he said. "Could you help, Greg?"

And suddenly they held her down, only two people but it felt like a dozen, restraining her. She tried to kick her legs, to flail out of here, no, not her baby.

"We have to cut it out of you," he said. "Now. If you don't struggle, it drastically increases your chances of survival."

"No!" she screamed. "No it's mine, please—"

"It'll only take a few minutes," he said. The doctor's face had disappeared, replaced by Schuller's. "We've found it here. And we can't let it get away." He drew closer to her, the razor sharp scalpel approaching her swollen belly. *No no no no no no no*

"No," she said, and she woke up, clutching her stomach. Her heart raced, and she remembered where she was. She rubbed her hands over her bare belly. No damage. No pregnancy. The nightmare lingered throughout the day.

Mary didn't tell anyone about Bart's behavior or his hallucinations, but it didn't help ease any tension in the camp. Schuller was running on little sleep, looking over thousands of lines of data, over and over again. He tried to find the lost particles, the name that had sprung up around camp for what they were searching for.

Helena hadn't reported back about her arm for two days. Mary heard Schuller roaring from Helena's lab as she went to check on her.

"Do it again!" he yelled.

"I've tested it five times, Doctor," she said, pleading. "Always the same results. The ice samples have nothing in them."

"I'm surrounded by morons, and cowards. I don't care how many times you've tested it. Do it again. Test it until we find something!" Spittle flew from his mouth, his skin sallow, his eyes sunken. He turned, saw Mary in the doorway, and stormed past her without a second look.

"I want it today, Dr. Darrow," he said, as he left.

Helena's arm was healing, but she was falling apart mentally. None of them were sleeping much.

"You need to sleep," said Mary, alone with Helena.

"I know," said Helena. "But we have so little time left. I know Dr. Schuller isn't being reasonable, but it doesn't matter. We have to exhaust all our possibilities. Try everything we can while we still can. Once we're gone, all we have is the data. And it's not enough. He won't get a grant next year, not after this. All of us will get more chances. He won't."

Mary left Helena to focus on her work. She checked on Bart, who was in his bunk, watching old movies.

"Anything to report?" she asked.

"Nothing," he said, half smiling. He looked optimistic. "Maybe it was just all this stress. Ever since I talked to you, no hallucinations, no bad dreams, no weird feelings. Sure as hell is still tense around here, but maybe I just needed a break. I'm ready to go home."

Mike found her later that evening.

"How's Bart?" he asked.

"Better, so far," she said. "Nothing strange to report from today."

"Good," he said. "I knew he'd be okay. This cold can make anyone crack. Are you ready to go?"

"I haven't decided if I am yet," she said.

"What?" he asked. "There's nothing here. We drill farther down, every day, and still nothing. Whatever Schuller thought he was going to find, it's not here, and probably never was. He sold his team a false bill of goods. Hell, sold himself it."

"It's not that," she said.

"Then what is it?" he asked. "We're all leaving. Jim told me he was opting out today. Got tired of Schuller screaming at him. That leaves only four and you, and I would bet that Jane and Helena aren't too far behind Jim."

"If I leave, it's over," she said. "Whoever stays, they need someone for emergencies. If they stay, they could die."

"That's exactly my point," he said. "You have to opt out. Once you do, they'll be forced to do the same. Why are they staying here? They're not getting anything more from that hole. They have their data. It can be examined anywhere. Schuller just doesn't want to admit defeat, and he wants to hold his team here, and endanger them. If you leave, it forces his hand, and *makes* him quit. He always gives up, in the end."

"What if he doesn't?" she asked. "What if he, and a few others stay? Say, Helena, Andrew, Jane, they all stay with him, and something happens. Another person gets left out in the cold for too long, gets worked too hard. I don't want their blood on my hands."

"It wouldn't be on your hands, Mary. It would be on his. It's all on him, not you. At a certain point, they're grown adults, and they can make their own choices, sink or swim. You're not God. You can't save everyone."

14

Mary didn't like Teddy. No one did. She hadn't understood Mike's dismissal of him at the poker game. The time she spent with him over the intervening days only proved Mike right, again. Teddy worked hard and did so consistently. He hung in Mike's crew because of his work ethic, because otherwise he acted like an utter asshole.

Not today. Today he was afraid.

Mary felt bad when he came to see her. He started having hallucinations the day before. He visited her in the morning. The chopper would arrive in two days.

"There's nothing physically wrong with you, as far as I can tell," she said. "All your vitals are normal. If we had any other kind of diagnostic equipment, I could do a blood or urine test. But your body is normal. When did it start?"

"Two nights ago," he said. "I had nightmares. Horrible, horrible nightmares. And I remember all of them."

"What were they about?" she asked.

He paused. "I'd rather not talk about it," he said.

"You can't tell me?" she asked.

"I'd rather not talk specifics," he said. "It was terrible. The worst I've ever had. I dismissed it, and went out on the ice, worked through the day. No real problems, until we got back last night. Then I started seeing colors."

"How?" she asked. "Randomly?"

"No," he said. "Coming out of people. Just colors, coming out of everyone's pores. They float in the air, like little clouds. As people walk around the base, they leave little trails, the colors sometimes mixing, mingling in the air. It was…beautiful."

"What colors?" she asked.

"All of them," he said. "It made for a nice change of pace on the ice. At first. All that white and gray was different."

"And it's with everyone?" she asked.

"Everyone," he said. "Everyone was colorful. Until they weren't."

"What changed?" she asked.

"At first, it was just colors. Mike was talking to me, and this brilliant navy blue started flowing out from behind him, like a cape, or wings. I didn't know what I was seeing. And I looked around, and the same was flowing from everyone on the dig. Came back here, same story. So I waited, trying to stay calm. We were all briefed on the mental effects of isolation, on being out so far. I never thought it would bother me. I've always been more of a loner. But I put it off, put it off, said I'd come talk to you only if it got bad.

I've never liked doctors. No offense. But then I was eating mess last night, and it got to where—where it wouldn't be sustainable."

"What happened last night?"

"There were still colors, dull greens, vibrant reds, neon yellows, but they weren't flowing out of the people anymore. They were the people now. Everyone was eating, wandering around, just floating clouds of color, flowing away in the wind. No people anymore. Just clouds. And I could still hear them and see their basic shape, but they weren't people anymore."

"What'd you do?" she asked.

"Nothing," he said. "I went to bed and hoped that it would be better in the morning. It wasn't. I talked to Mike, to see what he would make of it. I didn't get to say a word."

"Why?"

"I saw him, and I turned around, and came straight to you. This isn't tenable."

"What isn't?"

"The colors are gone, Mary. I was stupid to ever think it was okay, but the colors made it feel different. I thought maybe it was fine, because I was seeing things that were so beautiful. I'm tired of the ice. Tired of it. It all looks the same. You see all these photos of Antarctica before you get here, and it's these expansive vistas, of rising mountains and plains of snow. But it's all white and gray. Everywhere. The buildings are utilitarian. Everything has the color sucked out of it, worn away by the weather. I'm tired of it. Even when I watch movies, it feels like the color palette has been destroyed, evaporated. Like the continent has gotten into the screens—it makes me want to scream sometimes. But then there were the colors. And sure, it was crazy. But it was also beautiful. But I looked at Mike this morning. And you, now. It's the same."

What is the same?" she asked. He was rambling.

"The color is gone. You're all just gray, big gray blobs of smoke, but it's not just that either. I was stupid, so stupid. It was never clouds of vapor or smoke. That's just what it appeared, and I never looked closer. I didn't want to look closer, I couldn't, I knew, somewhere inside that if I looked, I would find out, and the illusion would disappear, but it's happened now, happened, and it will get worse—"

"Calm down, Teddy," she said. "Slow down. We're all gray now, but not smoke. What are we, then?"

He breathed in and out, his chest rising fast. "Sorry," he said. "I'm trying to stay calm, but it's hard."

She let him catch his breath. He turned to look at her, flinching.

"You're all insects," he said. "Tiny, tiny insects. Clouds of gray insects."

"That's what I am, right now?" she asked.

"Yes," he said. "I know it's you, underneath. But all I see is a swarm in your shape."

He's worse than Bart.

"I don't know what to do," said Teddy, looking away from her. "I can't live like this."

"Well, we don't know what's causing it," she said. "It might be the isolation, something like cabin fever, or it might be exposure to something in the drilling. Who knows? But the chopper will be here in two days, and you'll be on it. McMurdo has a much more advanced medical team. They will help you."

"I don't know if I'll make it two days," he said.

"First, no more drilling. No leaving the camp at all. Stay in your room as much as possible. I'll have Bill bring you your meals. If it's exposure to other people that's causing the hallucinations, that's causing the anxiety, then we'll limit it. Does it persist? Do they never go away?"

"Sometimes," he said. "But rarely. It feels like I'm breathing again when it turns off."

"Any funny feelings?" she asked. "Other than the hallucinations?"

"What do you mean, funny?" he asked. "I don't find any of this funny."

"Anything strange," she said. "Any feelings of disassociation or not being yourself."

"I don't think so," he said. "The hallucinations have been enough."

"Rest, and avoid as much stress as possible," she said.

"I'll try," he said. "What do I tell Mike?"

"I'll handle all that," she said. "Go lay down, and report back if it gets worse, if you think you're going to break down."

"Thank you," he said. "I'm sorry."

"Sorry for what?" she asked.

"Sorry for the way I am," he said. "I don't mean to be a dick. But I am. I've always been that way, prickly, obnoxious. Too smart for my own good. And I don't try to be that way. But I am anyway."

"It's okay, Teddy," she said. "It really is—"

"No, it's not," he said. "My nightmare—I always felt my nature was justified. I was smarter than everyone else. I saw what everyone else didn't, and that let me say anything I want. But in that nightmare, the first one, that started all of this, I knew I was justified, and I saw everyone, so dumb and slow. And I abandoned them to die. And I didn't think twice. I was superior. I need this to stop."

She dug through some shelves and found a bottle. She took a handful of pills and gave them to him.

"Sleeping pills," she said. "Two at a time. Sleep."

Teddy left, hopefully to sleep. The pills could be habit forming, but she'd worry about that later. She would have to tell Mike. But she would have to tell Schuller first. They couldn't run the drill with only two people, and now it was turning into an epidemic. Even if they were only his problem a couple more days, he needed to know. She would tell Mike after. It was her decision, not his.

Schuller would be in his lab. She walked there, passing through the empty common area and then the mess hall.

Bill was working, serving eggs and sausages. Beth drank coffee and ate, reading a book.

"Good morning, Miss Mary," he said, behind the counter. "Need any breakfast?"

He talked to her from her left side, and she caught a flash of light in her periphery.

"Sorry, Bill," she said. "Not hungry right now. Might come back for some in a bit." She looked at him now, as she walked, slowing down.

"I'll set you aside some," he said winking, sparks of light emerging from him, flying out of his mouth, his eyes. "Don't want Mike to eat it all." He winked again, and the sparks were brighter now. She froze, unable to speak.

"Something wrong?" he asked, and his eyes were only sparks now, whizzing, popping inside his skull. She blinked and they were gone, his big brown eyes back where they belonged.

"Sorry," she said, half-smiling. "It's been a rough morning. I have to go talk to Schuller."

"That'd put anyone in a rough mood," he said. "Good luck."

She went to leave, but then Beth waved her over. She walked over.

"How's Bart doing?" she asked, her voice low. "Mike told me something was up with him."

"He's okay," said Mary. *No, he's not. He's got company in his own body, and he thinks you're a monster, Beth. Thinks you're a giant bug. Teddy is joining him as we speak, can't even stomach looking at us.*

And Mary was next. "Just needs some rest."

"That's good to hear," she said. "Are you feeling okay? You look a little under the weather."

"I imagine it's all the stress," she said, Beth's face full of sparks and popping. Beth sat in an electric chair, wired with ten thousand volts. She *was* the electric chair, pure electricity coming with her voice, her eyes. She was energy. "I was just telling Bill, I have to go talk to Schuller."

"Are you planning on opting out?" she asked, her voice even lower. "You should. They need a push. He's holding his team here. Jim was the only one brave enough to join us." Her eyes bounced in their sockets, electric particles arcing back and forth, a tesla coil.

"I—I don't know yet," she said. "I"m sorry, I need to go." She left, walked away without a look back. She couldn't bear Beth's eyes. Small sparks, inside those dark holes, reflecting into her skull. What was happening to her? To them?

The nightmare of two nights ago. Put her on the same timeline as Teddy, but she only saw the hallucinations now. She hadn't thought much of the nightmare. She had thought it was only the stress bringing the old trauma back to the surface, one she had buried to survive. It was only the stress, only the stress.

No. There was something happening to them, three out of ten, all suffering from nightmares and hallucinations. She hadn't seen Bart yet today, but it didn't matter if he was recovering or not. This was too much of coincidence.

Something was happening, and it was happening to her, too.

15

Mary found Schuller bent over a lab table, studying something when she came in. He didn't turn as she entered.

"Please leave me," he said, without looking up. "No interruptions."

"We need to talk," said Mary, to his back.

"Ah, Ms. Jensen," he said. "Come to tell me you're leaving as well?"

"No—"

"Like rats from a sinking ship," he said, turning. No sparks and no light, thank God. He looked miserable, the color gone from his face, his eyes sunken. "Not that I can blame them. What have we gotten out of all this? One dead, two wounded. A career destroyed."

His manic energy had disappeared. He walked over to

his desk, his heels dragging across the floor. He looked as if he would collapse at any moment. He fell into his chair, gestured towards the chair in front of the desk for her.

She sat down. "People are getting sick."

"I know, I know, Ms. Jensen," he said. "I have eyes. I'm overworking them. Andrew nearly died, and now he's getting no sleep. Helena's hair is graying. Or maybe her dye is giving up the ghost. Either way. It's obvious this isn't working, even to me. Even the dig team is falling apart. Bart needed a day, and the man of stone, Mr. Hale, seems to be slowing down. It's my fault. It's all my fault. You were right, you know. About being a leader. Another thing those academics will never understand. Out here, it's different. You knew that. You've been a stranger in a strange land. I tried my best. Tried to lead by example. Tried to inspire people. Tried to mentor Andrew, and I only ended up nearly killing him. Another failure, in a long line of them."

Mary saw contrition in Schuller's face. He had given up. This would be another nail in the coffin.

"It's more than that," she said. "Bart came to me yesterday for a physical. He's suffering from delusions. Hallucinations. Severe."

Schuller's eyes widened. "What kind of hallucinations?"

"Off and on, he sees all of the crew as giant bug-like monsters," she said.

"Christ," he said.

"I put him on rest," she said. "And it has seemed to help. He's been in better spirits, and says the hallucinations have stopped, for now."

"Well, good," said Schuller.

"But I just left Teddy," she said. "And he's seeing things

too. It's more severe. He sees everyone—*everyone*—as clouds of tiny insects. I prescribed him bed rest and gave him sleeping pills to help."

"Both are seeing insects," said Schuller. "Any other symptoms?"

"They both had nightmares," she said. "Prior to the hallucinations. Bart described something else, something I can't explain. He talked about not feeling alone in his body, like he's sharing his skin with something else. Almost disassociative."

"And when did this start?" asked Schuller.

"Bart told me his first nightmare was Wednesday night," she said. "With the first hallucinations the next day."

Something changed in Schuller's eyes. A subtle shift. Later, Mary would identify it as the switch from defeat to hope.

"And Teddy?" he asked.

"A day later."

"And no others?" he asked, making eye contact.

"No," she answered, without hesitation. No others. She'd be fine. They'd be back in two days, back at McMurdo. She'd deal with the doctors there. Ones with no skin in the game. She could hold until then. They were just hallucinations. It was just too much pressure.

Under fire in Afghanistan, holding a man's arm together at an oil rig, on the water. You've seen pressure. This isn't pressure. It's inside *you*

Schuller leaned back, steepling his fingers.

"That's very interesting indeed," he said. "Two men, with similar symptoms. Any physical problems?"

"Nothing," she said. "That's the strangest thing. Both are perfectly healthy. The range of tests I can do here are narrow.

Once they get back to McMurdo, the doctors there should be able to do CAT scans, which could reveal something. Or it might be cabin fever."

"Right, McMurdo," he said. "Nothing else you can do for them?"

"Not right now," she said. "They need rest."

"Okay," he said. "I'd like to speak to them. Both of them, if possible, but especially Bart, considering he's patient zero."

"I mean, it should be fine," she said. "Teddy might be sleeping, but we can pay them a visit."

"I want to speak to them alone," said Schuller.

"Alone?" she asked. "Why?"

"Call it curiosity," he said. "I have a theory I would like to test, and I need to be alone. To eliminate variables. Also. Don't tell anyone else about this. I don't want anyone else knowing, not yet. It would only cause a panic."

"Okay," she said. "Are you going to talk to them now?"

"Yes," he said, getting up. "No rest for the weary."

"Then who's going out on the ice?" she asked.

"I think we're done there," he said. "I think we've reached its limits."

They went back to the main building, and Schuller made his rounds. Mary returned to her office. Mike stopped by.

"What did you tell him?" he asked, closing her door.

"I told him about Bart," she said. "And Teddy. He's seeing things too. That's two, Mike. He's the team leader. He needs to know."

"Teddy too?" asked Mike. "Jesus. What the fuck is going on?"

"I don't know," she said. "Schuller took it well. He seemed accepting about the whole thing, even about leaving. Maybe he finally realizes that it's over, time to move on."

"Said we're not digging anymore. What a relief," he said. "Maybe we can get some rest."

Mary didn't know how much sleep was in her future. She still saw Beth, sipping on coffee, bright sparks of energy bouncing around inside her empty eye sockets, buzzes and snaps filling the air as she talked. Schuller, scalpel in hand *we have to get it out of you*

Nothing but energy, nothing but matter

"Hopefully this will be the end of it," she said. "Hopefully we'll all opt out, and all go back."

Schuller visited her again, after speaking to Bart and Teddy.

"How were they?" she asked, them alone in her office.

"They seemed okay," he said. "If somewhat concerned. I did my best to reassure them. To let them know we'd get to the bottom of it. Are you staying with us, Ms. Jensen?"

"Staying?" she asked. "Transport will be here in two days. Less than two days. We're not digging anymore. Why would I stay?"

"Because we need you now, more than ever," said Schuller.

"We have two very sick men," she said. "We should all get back to McMurdo, before it gets any worse."

"But we can't leave, not after this breakthrough," he said. He smiled. The defeated look in his eyes had vanished entirely. They had sunken back into his skull, but he moved like a rested man.

"What are you talking about?" she asked. "We have two men on the edge of a psychotic break."

"No," he said. "Wrong. We have two men who are showing signs of first contact."

"What?" she asked.

"I know you've noticed it," he said. "You're smart, Ms. Jensen. And you've had to have noticed that Mr. Sizemore's first symptoms started right after we hit target depth."

"And?" she asked.

"And this is all the proof we need," he said. "The evidence we need to pivot. I was a fool. It was so simple, so plain in front of my eyes, but I never thought of it. I was so obsessed with the data, the data. Making sure those damnable sensors were aligned. Collecting ice samples. What was I thinking? I should have been a good scientist. A good scientist, when in doubt, would have returned to his hypothesis. My hypothesis was that an elementary particle was buried in the ice. In some sort of stasis. A particle that is responsible for turning us into what we are today. The jump-start to a new species, one with the intelligence to adapt, to grow. It would be unprecedented, unheard of, but I believed. But I attacked this problem using old methods. Old methods wouldn't detect something extraordinary. We didn't even know what we were looking for."

"I don't understand," she said. He spoke quickly now, words tumbling out of him, a dryer without a door, safety broken, spinning away.

"Bart and Teddy's behavior is no coincidence," he said. "In fact, it is *evidence*, evidence that we did find something down there in the ice. Our sensors didn't catch it, but we kept looking at the numbers, the data, trying to pull something from nothing. When we should have been looking elsewhere."

"But the sensors didn't show anything."

"The sensors were built to sense things we've encountered before. They wouldn't see these particles. I was foolish to think they ever would. I should have been thinking outside the box. Limited thinking. I won't allow it to happen again. We should have been looking in here," he said, pointing in his own chest. "If these elementary particles were the spark that created a species, where would they go, once awakened? They would go where they once were. Inside us."

Inside you

"And so I've changed my hypothesis, in face of this evidence," he said. "Chasing dead end data will get us nowhere. It is time to examine *us*, the new home of these particles."

"You want to examine Bart, and Teddy?" she asked. "We don't have the tools for it. McMurdo, or even a lab in the mainland—"

"I won't let them take my discovery away from me," he said. "And not just Bart and Teddy. They may be the only ones showing symptoms, but I believe that we've all been affected. Only Bill was absent from the dig site on that day, so perhaps he was too far to receive a spark, but everyone else, including myself, were there, at ground zero."

"But—"

"Tut tut," he said. His eyes gleamed with excitement. He had found his purpose again. "And that's why I'm here, Ms. Jensen. I want to ensure that you're staying with us. With your help, we can use that bare sliver of extra time and crack this nut."

"It's not responsible for us to stay," she said, her voice level. "It's not responsible for *you* to stay."

"Wrong again, Ms. Jensen," he said. "I would argue the exact opposite. We don't know what's inside us. It has caused

Mr. Sizemore and Mr. Ramirez to hallucinate, to question their very sanity. I would say it's our honest responsibility to examine what we have unearthed, and figure exactly its effect on us. Imagine bringing this back to McMurdo, and just giving them free rein with it. Don't forget, Ms. Jensen, the transport you flew in on to the base. It was an army vehicle. There is a government presence there and allowing them to tamper with the find of the century is irresponsible."

She imagined the thousand people at McMurdo, all seeing things, all hallucinating. Was it contagious? All it would take is one getting back—

No, this is crazy. She looked into Schuller's eyes. He believed.

"I can't promise anything," she said. "I'll decide tomorrow."

"Just think about it, Ms. Jensen," he said. "You were important before, for keeping us healthy and safe, but now you are integral. No one here has the medical knowledge you do. You'll be a part of the science team, as important as Andrew or Helena."

"Mark my words," he said. "We found something down there. And with your help, we can find out what it is."

16

Bart woke her up that night, coated in blood.

"Please help," he said. He carried Jane, her body covered in wounds, blood dripping off of her.

She scrambled, throwing on clothes and leading him to her office.

"Put her down there," she said, motioning towards her exam table.

"What happened?" she asked.

"I did it," he said, standing, his body limp.

"What?"

"I did it," he said. "I did it I did it I did it."

She grabbed a paperweight off her desk, ready to defend herself.

"Bart," she said, her voice hard. "Go back to your room.

Sit on your bed. Do not move. Do you understand?"

"Yeah," he said, and he walked away, out of the room. She needed help. She ran to Mike's room, glancing into Bart's room as she passed. He was sitting on the bed, staring down at the floor. It was a slaughterhouse in there and she was past it, at Mike's door.

She knocked. "Mike, I need help now," she said.

He answered in a second, bare chested.

"Wake up Jim and Beth," she said. "And tell them to keep an eye on Bart. They shouldn't try and talk to him, or engage him. Just keep him in his room. And then come to the exam room. I need your help."

"What's happening?" he asked.

"Jane is dying," she said, and she ran back to the exam room. Jane lay there, blood spilling from her onto the floor. *Get to work, Mary.*

She assessed the damage. Stab wounds all over her arms, defending herself. None in the legs, so the femoral was safe. Her torso was another story. She had several huge gashes in her stomach.

"Christ," Mike said, from the door.

"I need your help," she said. "Most of the wounds to her arms are superficial, but these wounds in her stomach need to be closed up. I need to check if there's internal damage and repair it."

"You're going to open her up?" he asked. "We have to wait for help."

"I have to try," she said. "Or she'll die before help arrives."

She grabbed the supplies she would need and set up a small workstation, handing Mike forceps, squeezed around antiseptic towels.

"I need you soak up any blood," she said. "I need to see my work."

She cut away of what was left of Jane's shirt, and saw her wounds. They were deep. She would cut near it, down into the abdominal cavity, and fix the damage inside. Mary knew it was Jane's only chance.

She grabbed the scalpel, and held it, her hand steady. She took a breath, looked at Mike, and then started to cut, firm pressure, blood welling up out of Jane's skin as she carved around the stab wounds, through skin and muscle. She moved fast, opening up an incision just big enough, peeling back the skin, fat, and muscle.

Disaster lay inside. Her intestines were shredded, rolls sliced open, bleeding out inside of her.

"Soak up all you can," she said, and Mike dabbed the towels, soaking up as much of the gore as he could. Mary got to work, trying to piece together her insides, stitching things back together, working as fast as she could. Jane's body was a timer.

She wiped sweat off with her sleeve, finishing the first suture, and beginning the second. Mike still pushed the towel through. There was less blood. Jane's blood pressure was dropping. Almost done. They could do a transfusion, but she had to seal her up first.

Then the light began to appear inside her. Jane's flesh disappeared, replaced by the globe lightning, electricity taken form. The organs in her hand disappeared and reappeared. Jane turned into energy before her eyes.

Not now, not now. She couldn't afford this. Mary closed her eyes, willed the hallucinations away. She would not be the reason this woman died.

She opened her eyes, and Jane was just flesh again.

Mary worked inside Jane, sewing up the internal injuries, her intestines in one piece again, if still in awful shape. But they would keep her alive until rescue came, and that's all she needed.

"Okay," she said. "Now to seal up the incision and the stomach wounds. Then to start the transfusion." She started stitching, over and over, she had to close the incision—

"Mary," said Mike.

"Wait," she said. She needed to finish stitching. Jane would die, the blood was everywhere—

"Mary," said Mike, louder.

"Wait, goddamnit," she said. "I'm almost done with this." Another few seconds and she'll be better, they could still save her—

"Mary," said Mike, grabbing her wrist, his strong grip only touching her. "She's dead. She's been dead for five minutes. She's lost too much blood."

Mike let go of her, and Mary fell back into her chair, her arms bloody up to the elbow. She held back her tears.

*

"What do we do?" asked Mike.

"We hold him in there, and we don't let him out," said Jim. "Your friend or not, he's a murderer. He's dangerous."

"Why didn't you tell us about his problems?" asked Beth, her face red from crying.

"Schuller told me not to," said Mary. "And he was getting better."

Only Teddy still slept. Schuller had gone to the comms to talk to McMurdo. Helena and Andrew went with him. Jane's body laid in Mary's office.

"Well he didn't stay better," said Beth. "What is going on?"

"Calm down, Beth," said Mike.

"Don't tell me to calm down," she said. "That's two dead! And what will happen to Bart?"

"I don't know," said Mike.

"I want to talk to him," said Mary.

"You what?" asked Jim. "He just killed someone. He's calm now, but who knows when he might flip back over."

"I need to know what he's thinking," said Mary. "He came to me, after he did it. He's afraid. I don't want him to hurt himself."

"It's your funeral," said Jim.

"I'll go in with her," said Mike. "We can keep him calm."

Bart paced back and forth in the small storeroom. They had let him clean off Jane's blood, and change clothes. He still didn't look like the Bart they knew. He stared down, his face contorted in anguish.

"Bart, will you sit down?" asked Mike, gesturing to the folding chairs in the corner. Bart realized himself, and grabbed one, unfolded it, and sat down. Mary and Mike remained standing. Mike glanced at Mary, a slight gesture with his head.

She stepped in front of him.

"Jane died, Bart," she said. "She bled to death. You stabbed her a dozen times. Do you remember doing that?"

"Yes," he said, tears welling in his eyes.

"Why did you do it?" she asked.

"Jane and I—" he started. "Jane and I had been hooking up for a couple months now. Just for fun, you know, nothing serious. She didn't want me to say anything to anybody. She considered it unprofessional. But we liked each other. She would wait until everyone was asleep, and then she would visit me. Said it was better that way. It was nice, knowing she'd be stopping in, in the quiet, in the dark. Made it feel less lonely."

"Bart—" said Mary.

"I should have told her," he said. "I should have told her about the hallucinations. She would have understood. She was smart. Smarter than me. So much smarter than me. But I was afraid, afraid she'd leave me in the dark, in the cold. It made me do it. Made me kill her. I didn't want to, but it kept making me see her as nothing, as less than nothing, as another obstacle, we're all obstacles—"

"Calm down, Bart," said Mike.

He looked up at Mike, and his eyes were frantic, darting. "Sorry, Mike. I'm sorry I fucked up."

"Tell us what happened," said Mary.

"She came over tonight," he said. "We watched Friends on my tablet. We had sex. We went to sleep. *She* went to sleep. I didn't sleep. I couldn't. That feeling, Mary. That feeling came back, worse than ever, stronger than ever. It filled me up with it, and I couldn't think straight. I tried to push it away, but it was there, and then she was lying next to me, asleep, but it wasn't her. It was a giant thing, a monster, a disgusting bug, and it was touching me. I fucked that thing, and it kept telling me and telling me—"

"What kept telling you?" asked Mary.

"I told you, I told you! My skin is a bucket, and it can only hold so much, and so much of me is just sloshing out, and it can't come back. There's so little of me left, and I can't feel myself, I can feel myself losing!"

"Breathe, Bart," she said. "Breathe."

He stopped, his chest rising, hyperventilating. He slowed his breathing.

"What's going to happen to me?" he asked.

"You'll be heading back to McMurdo," said Mike. "They'll figure out how you'll be tried. I think we're under Hawaiian authority officially, so they'll most likely have the FBI come and investigate—"

"No," said Bart. "No, not that. What's going to happen to *me*? You said they would fix me."

"The doctors will help you," said Mary. "At McMurdo. They'll do tests on you, and figure out what happened."

"They won't fix Jane," he said. "They can't. How will they get *me* back inside me?"

"I don't—"

"How will they get me back inside me?!?" he yelled. He started hitting himself, pounding his fists into his legs, over and over again. Mike stepped in front of Mary.

"Stop," said Mike, his hands out, palms down, trying to calm Bart. "Don't do that. We don't want you to hurt yourself." Bart stopped, his fists still balled in the air. He forced his palms open, looking at his hands, staring at them.

"I can't hurt myself," he said. "There's so little of *me* left. It's mostly *it* in here. It's a stranger, and I can't take it being in here anymore."

Bart stood up now, staring at Mike and Mary, back and forth, his head turning, back and forth, back and forth.

"Schuller told me—Schuller told me—"

"Schuller told you what?" asked Mary.

"He told me what it was—I don't want it inside."

"Bart—"

"You'll understand," he said. "Are you still Mike? Are you still Mike in there?"

"Yes, I'm still Mike," he said.

"How about you?" he said. "Mary? You talked to me, you caught it from me, do you still feel like you inside?"

"I'm still me, Bart," she said. She pleaded. "Please sit back down. Please calm down."

Bart reached into his pocket and pulled out a box cutter, and he extended the blade out a full inch.

"Whoa, Bart," said Mike. "Put that away."

"Stay back," he said, swinging it out in front of him. "I wouldn't hurt you Mike, but you know, I'm not me anymore. I don't want to hurt you. I want to just be me. You said they would fix me, Mary. You said they would fix me!"

He was screaming now, tears rolling down his face, as the two of them tried to quiet him down. They had locked the door behind them.

"They will fix you, Bart," she said. "But you have to give them a chance. Calm down. We don't want to hurt you. Put the box cutter down, and sit back down. I'll give you a sedative, and you'll wake up in McMurdo. You will be okay."

He was shaking his head, slowly at first, but then faster and faster.

"No, they can't fix me," he said. "They don't have medicine for this. I figured it out, while you were out there. Because I *am* a bucket. And there's only so much room in me. And I can't share it anymore. I can't—can't share it with the *something* anymore. And I can't get it out. There's just no way."

"Bart—"

"No, no, I can't get it out," he said. "But I can get *me* out."

He stabbed the length of the blade into his neck, under his right ear, and pulled hard left with all his strength, the metal ripping open his throat, blood pouring out of him. He collapsed on the ground in front of them, and died.

17

Mary told Schuller she was leaving later that morning.

No one slept after the attack. They had no more body bags, so they wrapped them in cellophane and put them in the freezer. Bill and Mike volunteered to help clean up. There was blood everywhere. Neither were squeamish, and it was sterile enough after a couple of hour's work.

There was no worry about destroying evidence. There was no question about what happened. There was only a dispute about why.

The immediate concern was about Teddy. He was a day behind Bart, but there were no sureties he wouldn't suffer a break the same way Bart did.

"I feel better," said Teddy. "Way better than I did yesterday. Maybe I just needed the sleep."

It was him, Mike, and Mary in his room, the door closed.

"That's what Bart told me too," said Mary. "Told me he was feeling better. No hallucinations. No funny feelings. And then he killed Jane."

"I don't think we're the same," said Teddy. "I mean, obviously, we're not the same. But I don't think we're being affected the same way, by whatever it is."

"You saw different things," she said.

"It's not that," he said. "I'm still seeing things. The hallucinations haven't stopped. But I feel more in control now. That's why I was so down when we talked, so worried. It would come and go, and then it just stayed, and I didn't know how to function like that. But now—it was a light switch before, but now it feels like my finger is on there, not someone else's."

"You can turn the hallucinations on and off?" she asked.

"Sort of," he said. "If I focus real hard, I can make it fade away. And it stays away. It's like looking at different layers of a painting."

"I don't think it was the hallucinations that set Bart off," said Mary. "He kept referring to something else inside him, something that was replacing him. And he couldn't get it out."

"I still feel like me," said Teddy. "I mean, when I say I feel better, I mean it. I'm not tired at all. Months of work, you get run down, no matter how much you rest. It's all gone. There's no voice inside, telling me to kill. I'm sorry about Bart, and Jane, I am, but I just feel…good."

"What did Schuller ask you?" asked Mary. He had talked to them both and hours later Bart was committing murder.

"How I was feeling," asked Teddy. "Where I was when we

hit target depth. If I would change my mind, and stay until the final bug-out date. I laughed at that. He didn't appreciate it, but he can fuck off. I want to go back to McMurdo, I want my head looked at, and I want my paycheck."

Mary blinked and his eyes were voltaic spheres. It was happening again, but no no, it was worse, his eyes went first, but soon his body changed as well, skin fading, translucent, veins, arteries underneath now electric lines, voltage running up and down, his electric eyes bouncing in his skull, no skull, just organs and blood, electric blood.

She couldn't look at him. Couldn't look at Mike. She closed her eyes. They still provided shelter.

"We want you to stay in your bunk until the chopper comes," said Mike. "Just to be on the safe side."

"No problem with me," said Teddy. "Knock on the door when we're leaving, and don't forget to feed me."

"You okay?" asked Mike, looking at Mary, her hands balled into fists at her side, her eyes closed. She didn't look at him.

"I need a break," she said. She opened her eyes, and it was back to normal.

They left Teddy and went back to her office. It smelled like a hospital. Like disinfectant and death.

"What's wrong?" he asked. She couldn't hide it anymore, it wasn't safe.

"Hallucinations," she said. "They started yesterday."

"Fuck," said Mike. "It's spreading. Whatever it is, it's spreading."

"I don't think it's spreading," she said. "I think we already have it. All of us."

"It?"

"I dismissed it," she said. "I noticed it with Bart, but I thought it was impossible. His first symptoms were the night that we hit depth. Me and Teddy started afterward. I wouldn't be surprised if someone else isn't reporting them. But everyone but Bill was there, on-site. And I don't know the range. He might have it too."

"What are you saying?" he asked.

"Schuller was right," said Mary. "There were particles. And now they're inside us."

"That's insane," said Mike.

"That's what Schuller believes," she said. "And I can't argue with him. Not anymore. It's too many coincidences."

"What about group psychosis?" asked Mike.

"I don't buy it," she said. "There hasn't been a collective trauma. There's plenty of people who spend months on the ice, and they don't all go crazy at once."

"What are you going to do?" he asked.

"I'll talk to Schuller, tell him I'm leaving tomorrow, and try and convince him to do the same. Andrew and Helena as well. This is too big for us. We need help. And if we leave them here alone—"

"They might tear themselves apart before transport comes for them," he said.

All three huddled together in his lab as she came in out of the cold. The wind howled outside. She hoped the chopper could still come tomorrow. They needed to leave.

"Ms. Jensen," said Schuller.

"We need to talk," she said.

"You're right," he said. "We do. Andrew, Helena, please leave us."

Andrew and Helena left. Helena gave her a fleeting

glance as she passed Mary. Mary couldn't place the look on her face. Whatever it was, Helena had chosen her side. She would stay with Schuller.

The door shut behind her, both of them back out in the cold.

"What did McMurdo say?" she asked. "About the attack."

"Oh right," he said. "They said—they said they couldn't get a chopper here any earlier than the already scheduled flight. Early tomorrow. I gave my statement. They will send an investigator out with the chopper."

"What did you say to Bart?" she asked.

"Excuse me?" he asked.

"You were the last one to talk to him," she said. "What did you say to him?"

"I believe Dr. Morroll was the last one to speak to him," he said.

"That's three dead under your watch, doctor," she said. "So be a smart-ass all you want, it's still on your hands."

He grimaced at that, and didn't hide it.

"I merely asked him how he felt," he said. "And for him to elaborate on the funny feeling he described to you. The bucket metaphor. I want to develop a test, to see if we can find the particles inside of those with symptoms. Are they in the blood, the brain? They could be in the spinal fluid. We don't know. All we have are the reports of those affected. So I tried to gather data."

"And six hours later he killed someone," she said.

"Under the effects of the particle," he said. "But Mr. Ramirez seems to be fine, in good health. Interesting results."

"Results?" she asked.

"Yes," he said. "We are the variables here, Ms. Jensen. Mr. Sizemore reacted poorly. Mr. Ramirez is reacting well, so far. This is what evidence we have of the particles. It is what we have, so it is what I will use to get more data."

"How can you talk like that when people have died?"

He sighed.

"As much as you want to paint me as a villain, Ms. Jensen, I did not kill anyone. Mr. Sizemore did that. Killed a very good young scientist, on top of it. Ms. Morroll and I did not always agree, but she was brilliant and had a bright future ahead of her. Mr. Sizemore seemed like a nice enough man, until—well, until he wasn't. But until we understand what we are dealing with, we don't know how to treat the people affected. This same particle led to our evolution! What effects could it cause in us today, versus the creatures we were a hundred thousand years ago? We could take another step, Ms. Jensen. And we could save lives to boot."

He glanced back at her, and his eyes were now electric. She didn't turn away, even as his body started to fade, transition into pure electricity. She couldn't run from them.

"I'm leaving tomorrow. I'm opting out," she said.

"No. You can't," he said. The current running through him intensified.

"Open your eyes, Doctor," she said. "The base was a butcher shop earlier. Our cook was cleaning up bloodstains. It will only get worse unless we leave. Whatever is in us—we can't handle it. We'll go to McMurdo and let them decide what to do with it. We are out of our depth."

"And give them the glory?" he asked. Schuller's body had vanished. Only energy remained. The electric skeins moved faster, up and down, his arms gesturing. "I found it and they laughed. I will not let this get away from me. You are mission critical, Ms. Jensen. You are as close to a medical doctor as we have. If you leave, it will only be us three. We need you."

"What you need is to stop this," she said. "We don't belong here. We should have never opened up that hole. We should have left it alone. None of this would have happened."

"I will not allow you to abandon us," he said, standing up, and he was human again, and he moved towards her. Mary reached into her pocket. She held the scalpel strong in her hand, ready. She held her ground. Rage filled his face.

"You've seen things, haven't you?" he asked. "I can tell. The way you look at us has changed. It is changing you, inside. If you stay, we can find out what."

"We leave tomorrow," said Mary. "And I highly suggest you and the rest of your team come with us. Abandon this. Rest. The science will still be there."

He blinked, and he backed up, paused, and sat down. "It won't be mine anymore. Please don't go, Ms. Jensen."

She let go of the scalpel in her pocket and left, without another word. Mary wouldn't argue any more. She had tried.

She found Helena in her lab.

"Hi, Mary," she said. "You're leaving, aren't you?"

"Yes," she said. "Please, Helena, come with us. There's nothing left here."

"I can't abandon him," she said. "He gave me a chance. Trusted in me."

"We are beyond any original scope of this project," she said. "If there is something inside of us, we cannot find it, or fix it. Your colleague is dead, Helena. That could have been you. It still could be you. Schuller is not stable anymore. All he sees is his discovery. Nothing else."

Helena's eyes closed, and then opened, and Mary thought she had changed her mind.

"I can't, Mary," she said. "I appreciate your care. But I made a promise, and I intend to fulfill it."

"He's dangerous," said Mary. "Your life is in danger while you're here."

"There's always a cost," she said, not meeting eye contact. Mary waited for more, but Helena said nothing else.

Mary retreated to her room, trying to make sense of everything, of what was inside her. Only hallucinations so far. But if Bart and Teddy's symptoms were prescriptive, she'd get the last stage soon. The disassociative feelings that Bart had felt. The feelings of strength that Teddy had.

How would it affect her?

She didn't know. The wind howled outside, the cold pushing against the walls of the building. They *didn't* belong here, out at the edge of the world. They had exceeded their bounds, pushed past the limit of man, and they had unlocked something they couldn't see, couldn't detect, and didn't understand. And it was inside of them, working its way through.

She leaned back against her pillow, the wind roaring. Exhaustion took over, and she slept.

A knock woke her up. What time was it?

"Come in," she said, and Beth opened the door.

"Aren't you coming?" she asked.

"Coming to what?" she asked. Was the chopper there? Had she slept through the night?

"You didn't hear? Schuller wanted everyone to attend," she said. "The last night of chapel."

18

There were eight of them at the last night of chapel, and all of them were electricity.

Teddy stayed behind in his bunk, like he promised, but the rest were there. Schuller wanted them all there. The only reason Mary attended was to present a dissenting opinion, to make one effort to get at least Helena and Andrew to come with them the next day.

And to keep tabs on Schuller, and his plans.

Mary couldn't adjust to the hallucinations, to the electric men that walked, moved around her. The zaps and pops as they spoke, as they touched anything. She flinched when Mike touched her shoulder, half expecting his lightning form to shock her.

They gathered. The vacant seats showed the loss. Jim sat

in the back row today, making his allegiance clear. The front row had Helena, Andrew, and three empty spots, including the one Schuller would sit in.

He stood in front of them, voltaic.

"I know we've suffered some setbacks, some tragedies. But if this is the last time that we assemble as a team, I want to congratulate everyone on the things we have achieved, and thank you for your efforts in those achievements. We will follow normal protocol, however. Helena?"

The line of electricity gestured towards another, and Helena stood up in front of them.

She spoke in lines of current and voltage.

"First, I want to have a moment of silence, for the losses of Bart and Jane. It was a truly tragic incident, and we should honor their memory."

The room went silent, and Mary closed her eyes.

She was trying to breathe.

"Keep breathing, honey," said Greg, as he rushed them to the hospital. Her water broke in the middle of the night. It was time to have their baby.

No no, this didn't happen. We never got this far—

She breathed small, short breaths, like her instructor told her to. She still had some time, but she felt the pressure of the baby. She didn't want to give birth in a car.

"Tell me everything will be alright," she said, focusing on her breathing, the seat reclined all the way back.

"Everything will be alright," he said, holding her hand, smiling. "We're going to have a little boy."

They got to a hospital and got her a room. It smelled like disinfectant and death. Her contractions came closer and closer, and her anxiety compounded every time, her worry building inside her.

This never happened—

She reminded herself, this is parenting. It's caring about another person, one you helped create. One you carried. One that grew inside you.

Greg helped, reassuring her, bringing her whatever she needed. He wanted to be there, the whole time. He couldn't carry the baby, but he could support her. She loved him.

Then it was time. Dr. Stevenson would bring their baby into the world. He stood ready. The nurse stood nearby.

"Seems like your little boy is about ready to join us," said the doctor. "I want you to concentrate on your breathing, and when I say push, I want you to push."

She breathed, her heart racing, the pressure of the baby enormous.

"Push," he said, his voice loud and firm.

She pushed, her breath in and out, in and out, her hand clamped down on Greg's. He squeezed back.

"Breathe," he said. She focused on her breathing.

"Now push," he said, again. She could feel it get closer.

"Now focus on your breathing," he said, and she did, breathing like her coach told her to, small, short breaths and *she was never here, this never happened.*

"Just one more should do it. Push," he said, and she pushed, and the baby left her, a great gasping emptiness inside her where it once was. She had succeeded, bringing it into the world. She felt tired, overjoyed, sad, everything, all at once.

Dr. Stevenson held it in his arms, toweling it off, wrapping it.

"Oh, it's beautiful," he said. "Truly one of a kind. Would

you like a look, Mr. Hoffman?"

Greg let go of her hand, and walked over to the doctor at the foot of the bed.

"It's gorgeous," he said, smiling at it, and then at Mary.

"Please, let me see," she said. "Let me hold my baby."

"Of course sweetheart," said Greg, taking the swaddled baby from the doctor, carrying it over to her. "Look at what we've made."

He handed it to her, and she held it on her breast, and saw it for the first time, and she couldn't breathe.

She held an insect, a giant aphid, legs scrambling in the air, multi hinged carapace, mandibles chewing.

"Good job," he said, caressing the creature's head.

"Where's my baby?" she asked. "This isn't mine, this isn't mine."

"You made it, sweetie," he said. "It grew inside of you."

She opened her eyes, and everyone was human again in the common room. Helena had finished, sitting back down. Andrew took her place. Mary looked around, trying to clear her head, her heart racing, her breath coming in ragged gasps. Mike glanced at her with concern, and she waved him off. Another vision. Waking now. It was getting worse.

Andrew stood in front of them, looking better than he had in days. He had recovered from his bout with death. He glowed now, his skin warm, his lanky frame full of energy.

He presented the last of his findings. It said nothing, and everyone knew it.

The five of them in the back row sat in silence. She could feel the tension in Mike sitting next to him, and she knew he wasn't listening to any of this. He waited for Schuller to talk.

Schuller stood up. He turned off the projector and put

the lights back on.

"I don't need any slides today," he said. "I know most of you have made up your minds. But please hear me out. It's a been a long season, with our share of tragedies, and all of us working ourselves to the bone, trying to succeed."

He stood up straight, his voice firm, his fingers moving again. Just like he was on the verge of target depth. He believed again.

"And we were on the precipice of failure. But that's all it was, the precipice, because we looked over the edge, and then we turned back, because we haven't failed. We have succeeded, succeeded beyond our wildest dreams."

She could hear Mike's breathing speed up next to her. Schuller continued.

"Because we found something, down in the ice. All that time, I had doubts, doubts about my hypothesis. I had doubts, that maybe I reached too far. That thinking we'd find a new elementary particle, something new, something that would upset the apple cart that was established science was too big an idea, too radical. But I was wrong because I did not dream big enough. We have found something else, something even bigger, more momentous."

"We dug into the ice, to unearth these hidden particles, but they couldn't be seen, couldn't be counted. None of our sensors saw them, and so we presumed failure." He raised a finger into the sky.

"Wrong, wrong, wrong. They are still hiding, but now, they hide inside us. They belong in us, as a part of us. It is the reason we became homo sapiens, and I believe that all of us are on the path to the next step, the next level of evolution. They are in us now. We no longer have to look into the ice to find the spark. We just have to look inside ourselves."

Andrew sat rapt with attention, his back straight, on the edge of his seat. Helena sat next to him, looking up at Schuller, her eyes gleaming. They ate it up. They wouldn't leave him.

Schuller moved faster now, pumping his fist with every word, his voice raising in volume until he was nearly shouting.

"And if we go back," he said. "That will all be taken from us. We will lose our discovery. We will lose all our hard work. And we will lose our freedom. Because they won't care about any of us anymore."

"So, I'm begging you, stay. It is not too late. With just another few weeks, we can forestall winter and we can discover ourselves what we have inside us. We can isolate it, learn, and solve its riddle. Stay. Do not do it for me, but for yourself. This is the defining moment of all our lives, and we cannot flee from it, like cowards. We must be brave, and face it, even in the threat of fear, of winter, of ice. Do it for yourselves, and do it for our fallen comrades, Jane, Bart-"

And with that, Mike, whose breath had quickened, whose fingers were digging into his legs, got up, moving through the chairs in front of him. He charged Schuller, and Schuller had no chance. Mike grabbed him in his arms and knocked him to the ground without effort. He started hitting him. Schuller tried to block the vicious punches, but they only stopped some damage.

Mike would kill him. As he swung, he shouted, loud barbarous roars of pain and anger.

"You don't say his name! He was a kid, and you pushed him, pushed him to kill! You can't feel that guilt? Then I'll give you something you can!"

Mike's words soon became just expressions of raw anger and violent noise, as he struck Schuller again and again, and then they were pulling him away, their arms wrapped around his waist, anything to make him stop. Mike had endured Schuller's command and carelessness for months and it had boiled over. Mike had reached his breaking point.

"You'll kill him," said Mary. "Stop, please." `

"It's what he deserves," said Mike. "Look at him, begging for us to kill ourselves for him." He was yelling at Helena now, Andrew. "You don't see it? He'd sacrifice all of us just for that little bit of glory he keeps talking about, even if it's inside his own head. I'm glad you're staying, Schuller, because if I see you again, I'll kill you. I hope you're ready for prison, because all these deaths will be put on your head. I'll make sure of it!"

Helena and Andrew pulled Schuller up, who bled from his nose and mouth. He was lucky he was still conscious. They helped him away, leading him back to his lab.

Mike calmed down, and they let go of him.

"That son of a bitch," he said. "I swear to Christ—"

"Mike," said Mary. "You're not helping anything."

"I don't care," he said. "I just wanted him to shut the fuck up for once."

With Mike calm, they retreated to the mess hall, where Bill gave them the rest of a cake he had made the day before.

"This is the last food I'm making in Antarctica," he said. "So you better damn enjoy it. Feel sorry for them staying behind. Won't have my excellent cooking to get them through the cold."

"I hope you were serious about visiting your mom," said

Mary. "I want some of that home cooking."

"Oh you know I was," he said. "As soon as we get home." He smiled, his eyes closed.

The mood lightened, if barely, a light at the end of the tunnel. The wind howled outside, but it had slowed since the night prior. All forecasts had the chopper arriving on schedule, the worst weather holding off. They ate their cake and Mary helped Bill clean the kitchen for the last time.

They all went to get ready, and pack the few things they had. She finished, and walked the main building, making sure she hadn't missed anything. She saw Mike, sitting next to the body of Bart. She thought to say something, but she left him alone and let him have his grief.

Mary waited for more visions that night, more hallucinations, more nightmares, but none came, and she slept that night with no interruptions. The chopper arrived in the morning, early.

She knocked on Teddy's door. He was already awake, dressed, looking healthy.

"Chopper's here," said Mary. "Ready to take us home."

"Great," he said. "We can finally get out of this shithole."

19

The chopper landed on schedule. Alex had no investigator on board.

"Bodies? More of them? Plural?" she asked, the blades spinning down behind her, as she and Mary walked into the main building.

"Should have gotten a call yesterday," said Mary. "Early. A murder-suicide."

"First I've heard of it," she said. "We haven't had any contact since you scheduled the chopper."

"That lying bastard," said Mary. "Schuller was supposed to keep McMurdo updated."

"Well, he didn't," said Alex. "Jesus, it's a real shit show here."

"You're telling me," she said. "We have two dead bodies,

and five live ones, ready to go."

"As soon as we load up, we can leave," she said. "Another bad storm rolling through later today, so we should get in the air as soon as possible."

"We'll get everyone organized and load up," she said.

She found Mike and Beth, talking in the mess hall.

"Schuller didn't radio in," said Mary. "They didn't know about Jane and Bart."

"Should have known it," said Mike. "He's been hiding his incompetency from anyone who can do anything."

"Has anyone seen him since last night?" asked Mary.

"He's holed up in his lab," said Mike. "As far as I know. Leave him there to rot. I'll be happy if I never see him again."

Her things were packed. Mary went around camp, checking on everyone. Teddy's room was bare, and he was sitting on the edge of his bed.

"How are you doing?" she asked.

"Better than ever," he said, smiling. It was wide and genuine. She didn't think she'd seen Teddy smile in the few weeks she'd been here.

"No hallucinations? No visions?" she asked.

"I told you, I'm in control," he said. "I can't explain it. I feel great. Ready to get the hell out of here."

"We'll be loading up soon," she said.

"Ready when you are, captain," he said.

Mary found Beth packing hastily.

"I half want to just throw all this shit away," said Beth, rolling t-shirts and stuffing them into a duffel bag. "It feels tainted. This wasn't what I imagined this job would be like. In and out, one long summer season, work in the cold, see some sights, and then get back. Wasn't expecting this."

"I don't think anyone did," said Mary. "I thought this would be an *escape* from shit."

"Ha," said Beth. "Fucking right."

"Just think," said Mary. "A few rides away from home."

"Ready for my own bed," she said. "And to see my dog."

Jim and Bill each held a beer in the empty kitchen, laughing at something.

"Seems like you two want to stick around," said Mary, walking in on them.

"Oh hell no," said Bill. "I didn't sign up for no crazy particles putting up stakes in this 'ole homestead."

"Couldn't have said it better myself," said Jim, following it with a swig. "I came here to study ice, not people."

"And I came here to study ice too…ice cold beer," said Bill, with a burst of laughter.

"Don't drink too much," said Mary. "We're heading out soon, trying to stay ahead of the weather."

"Don't you worry, Miss Mary," said Bill. "I'll keep an eye on Jim, keep him in control. But then again, I ain't flying the helicopter, am I?"

Mike stood near the bodies, in the corner of the freezer. Mary wore only a long sleeved shirt, but the air inside the freezer felt temperate. After enduring temperatures of below -50, just below freezing felt damn near pleasant.

"I don't even know where his parents live," said Mike.

"Iowa," she said.

"I need to tell them," he said. "They deserve that, at least. He deserved more. How did it come to this?"

"It's my fault," she said. "I should have done more."

"Hey, you didn't make him go out on the ice," he said. "We couldn't have known. How are you hanging on?"

"It's getting worse," she said. "Bouts of hallucinations last longer and longer. I don't know what they'll do with me once we get back."

"It's still a damn sight better than staying here," he said. "Just have to hold it together a little while longer. McMurdo can handle anything."

She returned to her room, sat down, and breathed. Mary closed her eyes. The cold, the lack of sleep, the visions, and the death piled on top of her. Walking weeks without a safety net in case she fell. Bart had fallen, and he took Jane with him.

They were dragging her out onto the ice. Out to the hole.

"It's for your own good, Mary," said Mike, holding her wrist. Jim held another, Beth and Bill her ankles. The wind whipped through them at the dig site, cutting through them like box cutters, box cutter blades through Bart's throat, his neck opening wide, a second smile, blood pouring out of him.

She didn't feel the cold. Not like she used to. It didn't hurt or numb. It was simply present. She had become a part of it.

"Let me go," she said, struggling. Their grip held like iron, too strong to break, no matter how hard she struggled.

"Real sorry to be doing this, Miss Mary," said Bill, looking at her in the eyes. "But you've become one of them now. You don't belong with us anymore. It's better this way. Can't take you back. Might spread, you know."

"Mike, please," said Mary, begging.

"You're not really Mary anymore," he said. "So that's not going to work. I knew the real Mary. You're not her."

They approached the drilling equipment. But they had moved it back. They had dug the hole, gotten what they needed out of it. The team had awakened the thing that was down there, the lost particles, the god particles. The hole was still open, still a gaping maw, three feet wide, the fading light of blues, darkening as you looked down, down, down.

She struggled, but it was no use. They wouldn't listen. All made of steel, unwilling to bend. They would take her to the hole and put her down in the ice where she belonged.

"Please, don't do this," she said.

"We could have just killed you," said Jim. "Mike said this was more humane. Put you back where you came from. Catch and release, so to speak."

"Biggest fish I've ever caught," said Bill, laughing.

"You can't fool us anymore," said Beth. "We've seen the real you. The real Mary would have already froze to death."

They were all bundled up, layer after layer of thick winter gear, their hoods drawn up, fur-lined parka and scarf after scarf, covering and obscuring their faces. She looked down at herself. She realized she was only wearing a thin long-sleeved shirt and her work scrubs. She should be frozen. Beth was right. She felt the cold, but it didn't hurt her.

They arrived at the hole.

"You can jump," said Mike. "Or we can throw you. It's your choice."

"Please, not down there," she said. "Please, I can't. I can't."

"Then we throw you," he said.

"No, please," she said, tears welling in her eyes, not freezing. "I'll jump. Please let me go."

They dropped her on the hardened ice. Frozen hard, solid, for thousands of years. It had never thawed, not until they arrived, not until man had paved the way. He had warmed the air and softened the ice just enough. Just enough for them to send out a warning call, a burst of signals to bring man here, to bait man into digging them up. So they could again be inside. They had endured the cold for so, so long.

"What are you waiting for?" asked Mike with no mercy in his eyes. They surrounded her. Her terror would eat her alive, and they would grab her, throw her. She tried to run anyway. She had to try. She wouldn't go back down there, not willingly.

They grabbed her, and she screamed and then they tossed her. Her legs scraped against the edges at the top and then she fell. She bounced off the sides, the distance immeasurable, but still falling. She had to stop, or she would die. She stuck out her feet, no room to maneuver, such a small space, and it hurt, but she slowed, and she pushed out harder, the ice grinding away at her. She caught herself, slowing down, sliding down the tube, no light visible above, so far down. She slid down, down, and she was at the bottom. Where they started.

She looked up and there was nothing, not even a glimpse of the dim sun above. She breathed what little breath she could. Mary felt the weight of the ancient ice around her. The ice pressed in, cracking around her, as it refroze. It wouldn't stay open forever; it would entomb her, entomb them again, trap them again in the ice. No it had been too long, much too long. She must take them out; she must survive. She wouldn't be buried, she wouldn't die down here in the ice. They had a kinship in that.

They wouldn't die in the ice. They would return, they would persist. She would persist. Partners in survival.

She started to climb, jamming the metal spikes in her boots into the sides of the tunnel, pushing herself up, step by step. She would get out of here, out of this hole in the ice, and she would show them their mistake. They would show them their mistake.

"Ms. Jensen," said someone, a voice around them, coming from the ice. The ice did not talk. They had spent millenia down here, trapped. The ice had stayed mute, utterly careless in its quiet.

"Ms. Jensen," the voice said again, and she was in her bed.

She jumped, the voice pulling her out of her nightmare.

"Ms. Jensen," said the voice. It came from Schuller, skulking, wary. His swollen lip affected his speech. As he came out of the shadows, she saw his bruised face, both eyes blackened. Even injured, he wouldn't stay still, his eyes moving, maybe looking for Mike, worried about getting another beating.

"What do you want?" she asked.

"You're having visions," he said. "You understand better than anyone now. How does it feel? Can you feel them inside you yet? Can you feel them changing you?"

"Leave me alone," she said. "Go back to your lab, go back to your science. We're leaving. If you were smart, you'd leave now."

"I can't leave," he said. "I can't go back. There's nothing for me back there. Everything I need is right here."

Nothing held Schuller to reality anymore. Mary didn't know if anything would bring him back. If he stayed, he would never return.

"We need you," he said, again.

"You've told me," said Mary. "But I don't care about your mission. I've done all I can to help."

"But you haven't!" said Schuller, growling. "You haven't done a thing but run away. We're on the verge of something, something big. Without you, we will fail."

"You've already failed," she said. "You have failed by every possible metric."

"No," he said. "Not yet. This is your last chance. I won't let you leave."

"Try," she said, standing up to him, moving towards him. He cowered, and then fled, disappearing down the hall, and out of sight.

20

They loaded the bodies first, in the rear compartment of the big helicopter. Mike insisted on helping carrying Bart. Everyone else followed, loading up their gear, stowing their meager belongings. The wind picked up again. They needed to leave.

"How we looking?" asked Mary.

"Five by five," said Alex. "No problems, as long as we get in the air within the hour. I would like to get back to McMurdo. It's enough of a hellhole as it is. How many are we transporting?"

"Five," said Mary. "Not counting the bodies."

"And the rest?" she asked.

"They're staying," said Mary. "For the final bug out date."

"Risky," said Alex. "As the weather gets worse. They

might be in for a long winter out here."

"Don't get me started," said Mary.

"I saw a lanky fellow out here a little while ago. He was outside, loitering around. You know why?" she asked.

"That'd be Andrew," she said. "One of the stay-behinders."

"He beat it when he saw me walking back out to the chopper. Don't know why anyone would be out in this cold for longer than necessary."

Mary wore layer after layer, bundled up, like everyone else, to keep out as much of the cold as possible. To stop hypothermia and frostbite. No amount of layers would suffice. The cold would still get in.

But Mary felt fine. She felt the cold, felt its presence. Everyone else moved in and out of the main building, carrying their gear, the few bags they packed. They hustled back inside until it was time for final departure. Alex herself looked miserable as she followed through final checks on her vehicle.

But Mary could have stood out here for hours. And she knew why.

The timeline worked out. She had started seeing things two days after Bart, one day after Teddy. Whatever it did to Bart, he couldn't take. It drove him insane. It had the opposite effect on Teddy, his normal glowering self changed, his weariness gone, his self awareness up. He was a new man. What part of it was the particles? She didn't know.

But she knew the cold didn't affect her anymore. She could strip down to her underwear and lay down on the ice, and it wouldn't do a thing. The thought scared her. It wasn't right, wasn't human. Was she human anymore? The

visions and hallucinations all told her no, but she didn't believe them. She couldn't, didn't know what the changes in
her brain, her physiology meant. She didn't want to know.
Mary knew going back to McMurdo would have them investigate. Have them find out. And God knows what would
happen to her there.

Were there others, seeing things, dismissing them, just
trying to keep sane long enough to get back to McMurdo?
After Bart, no one was talking. Maybe they were discover-
ing new things about their bodies, just like Mary. Were they
all good?

She didn't fear the cold anymore, but she still wanted off
the ice.

Mike found her in her room, surprising her.

"I'm goddamn tired of being surprised," she said.

"Sorry," he said. "I didn't mean to."

"I know, I know," she said. "Schuller snuck up on me earlier. Tried to get me to stay again. I blew up at him."

"Good," said Mike. "Fuck him."

"I don't think there's any coming back for him," she said.
"The look in his eyes. It looked like betrayal."

"You starting to feel sorry for him?" he asked.

"It's pity or hate," she said. "And hate's not healthy."

"We didn't betray him," said Mike. "He couldn't handle
it."

"It didn't just look like he thought we betrayed him," said
Mary. "It sounded like life had betrayed him."

"He doesn't know real loss, so when an impostor comes,
he takes it at its word."

"Soon we'll be off the ice," she said.

"I'm sorry," he said, without prompting.

"Always apologizing," she said. "Sorry for what?"

"Bringing you out here," he said. "Into this storm of bullshit. I thought it would do you good."

"I thought it would too," she said. "Get away from everything. Get away from the city. See a new place and put my nose down and work."

"Instead, we got lost particles and crazy doctors," said Mike. "Let's get the fuck out of here."

Alex gave them the go ahead and they hustled through the cold, a line of bundled figures moving back and forth between the main building and the helicopter. Alex started the chopper, getting the engine warm. The vehicle filled up and soon they were ready to go. Panic hit Mary. She had forgotten her last bag.

"Shit," said Mary, speaking into Alex's ear, over the roar of the blades and engine. "Still have one bag inside. I'll be right back."

She hurried into the main building. Only needed to grab her last bag. The roaring wind, the spinning blades of the chopper disappeared once she went inside. She walked to her room, and then caught something out of the corner of her eye, a glimpse of something moving. She looked up to see Helena turn a corner at the end of the hallway. Mary called to her.

"Helena, wait," said Mary. "It's not too late. Come with us." Her voice echoed down the hall, but there was no response, and Mary didn't pursue her. Helena didn't want to be saved.

She ducked into her room. Her duffel bag sat on the foot of her bed. She did one last quick glance around, but nothing stood out. Oh well, she would have left it all behind if it meant getting on that chopper. She turned back to her bag, to grab it, but it was open, the flap loose. She had closed it before leaving it. Someone had rifled through it. She looked inside.

There was nothing missing inside, only a folded over piece of notebook paper on top of everything, just set there. She unfolded it. It had one word written on it, in big block letters.

BOMB

Helena had left the note.

Schuller's last words.

"I won't let you leave."

She ran.

She ran toward the exit, towards the chopper. They would all die.

She sprinted through the empty building, her footsteps echoing, and then she hit the outside, the helicopter blades spinning. She ran toward them over the ice, the spikes in her boots crunching. She waved her arms in the air, hoping someone would see her, someone would realize something is wrong.

"There's a bomb!" she screamed. "There's a bomb in the helicopter!"

She screamed as loud as she could, but she could barely hear her own voice. She saw Mike see her, say something, and get out of the chopper, running to her. Teddy looked confused and got out after him.

"There's a bomb! There's a bomb! Everyone needs to get out!" she screamed, as Mike got closer.

"What?" he yelled, over the din of the wind and the chopper.

"There's—"

The helicopter exploded.

21

The explosion threw Mike to the ground, a burst of force and fire.

Mary saw this before being knocked down by the strength of the blast. She felt shrapnel fly overhead, but nothing hit her.

Mike.

Mike was moving towards her when it exploded. She looked, saw his body face down in front of her. He moved. She ran towards him, smoke and metal everywhere.

She crouched next to him. No damage to his back. She rolled him over, and he wasn't hiding any injuries there either. They were lucky. He looked at her, confused.

"Mike," she said.

"What happened?" he asked. "Was that the chopper?

Something hit me in the head."

Mike's eyes stayed dilated as she talked to him. He had a concussion. She felt the back of his head, but only felt a large goose egg, no lacerations.

"They planted a bomb on the helicopter," she said. "To keep us here."

"They've gone insane," he said. "I'll—"

"Stay still for now," she said. "I'm going to look for other survivors."

She walked through a nightmare. The chopper had exploded, the engine and bits of the metal shell flying in all directions. The people in the cabin and Alex—Mary had seen bombs hit vehicles in Afghanistan. She seldom saw survivors.

Pieces of metal smoldered everywhere, the core of vehicle still in one piece, but destroyed and on fire. She looked around the periphery before she went to the cabin itself. She tried to hold out hope that anyone would survive.

She heard grunting, and followed the sound to a huge piece of wreckage, covering someone trying to pry their way out from underneath it. She ran over, and saw that it was Teddy. He had found his way out of the chopper moments before it exploded. It had saved his life.

Teddy," she said, and grabbed the edge of the piece of metal, getting it off the ground, and then upending it off of him.

"What the fuck," he said. "Mary. What the hell is happening?"

"A bomb," said Mary. "To keep us here."

"What the fuck?" said Teddy, again.

"What hurts?" she asked. They had to save who they

could now. They could worry about Schuller later.

"My ribs," he said. "My leg."

She looked over his torso, not easy with the layers of clothing, but there were no perforations of his parka. She touched his torso, pressing through to his body, and he barked in pain when she felt his lower right side.

"Broken ribs," she said. "Which leg?"

"My left," he said. She didn't need detective skills to diagnose it. A jagged shard of metal protruded from the meat of his calf. She would need to remove it, stitch up his wound.

"You have a piece of shrapnel in your leg," she said. "We need to get you inside."

"I'll be fine for now," he said. "Check everyone else."

She didn't know if there was anyone else to check, all the others being inside the chopper when it exploded. Mary walked toward the burning wreckage, afraid of what she would see. She found exactly what she expected.

The bodies of her friends.

Alex still sat in the pilot's seat, not moving, her features unrecognizable. Beth, Jim, and Bill all sat in the cabin itself, and she looked for them, hoping that maybe they survived. Hoping for a miracle.

She checked Beth's pulse, her body blackened by the explosion. Nothing, her skin charred. The explosion had ripped through her. It had killed her instantly. She went to poor Jim next and he was burned as well. He been sitting closest to the fuel tank, and he hadn't stood a chance. It had ignited a foot away from him. He had absorbed most of the blast. His arms and legs had been blown off, strewn somewhere in the wreckage.

She checked Bill last. His skin was burnt, ash all over

him. He had no legs, one gone below the knee, one just above. The force from the fuel exploding had torn a piece of metal loose from the shell of the vehicle and it had ripped his legs off on its way. She reached for his pulse, expecting nothing.

He gasped when her hands touched him.

"Jesus," she said, startled. He was still alive. If they could stabilize him, if they could stop the bleeding, she could save him. She had seen worse of men who survived because they acted quickly. She moved.

"Bill," she asked. "Can you hear me?"

"Yeah, Miss Mary," he said, opening his eyes. "I don't feel right."

"You're in real bad shape," she said. "I need to move you, and it will hurt like hell. I need you to try and stay conscious."

"I'll try, Miss Mary, I'll try," he said, his eyes barely open. "What happened?"

"The helicopter blew," she said.

"Just my damn luck," he said. "That's what my momma always said. Said I was born under a bad sign. Only good thing came out of it was me knowing how to make some good biscuits."

She cut through the remains of the restraints from the seat, burnt in tatters, and put her arms under his armpits, hoisting him out of the aircraft. Even without his lower legs, Bill was heavy. Mary's back screamed as she pulled him out. Bill moaned in pain.

"Stay with me, Bill," she said. "Stay with me."

"I'm trying," he said. "Where'd my legs go?"

"Let's worry about keeping you alive," she said. "We'll

stop the bleeding and then get you inside." She laid him down on the ice, and pulled off her belt. She tied it around his thigh, as tight as she could pull. Bill moaned again.

"It's too much, Miss Mary," he said. "It's too much."

She grabbed his hand, and squeezed it. He squeezed back.

"One more leg," she said. "I'm going to take off your belt."

"I didn't even buy you a drink," he said, his words rough.

She pulled off his belt and wrapped it around his other thigh, pulling it through and tight, as tight as she could. The ice was already stained with the blood coming from the blasted wounds where his legs used to be.

"Now we're going to take you inside," she said. "Still with me?"

"I'm so tired," he said. "So tired, Miss Mary. This god-damn cold. Please don't let me die in the cold."

Mike appeared out of nowhere.

"You shouldn't be helping," she said. "Your head—"

"We don't have time for head trauma," he said. "I helped Teddy inside."

"They could be waiting for him," she said. "Schuller and his inner circle."

"If they wanted to finish us," he said. "They would have already done it."

Mary took off her parka and laid it on the ground.

"What are you doing? You'll freeze," said Mike.

"We have to carry him somehow," she said. "Help me put him on it."

They grabbed Bill and laid him on Mary's parka.

"Still with us, Bill?" she asked. His eyes flickered open. "I need you awake. Even if it hurts."

"I'm awake, I'm awake," he said. "It hurts."

"Let's go," she said, and she and Mike carried Bill, holding the parka as a makeshift sling, the thick fabric supporting what was left of Bill's body. They carried him away from the wreckage. The bodies would have to wait. The wind howled even harder. The promised bad weather had arrived, and they needed to get Bill inside. A trail of blood followed them as they carried him in, back to the relative warmth of the base. Teddy leaned against a wall inside, a small pool of blood around his injured leg.

"I didn't want to go any farther in," he said. "Can't trust those fuckers."

They looked up and down the corridors. Listened. Nothing. No sounds at all, no trace of Schuller or his circle.

"We don't have time," said Mary. "Let them come." They grabbed Bill and moved, with Teddy limping after them. They moved to Mary's office.

Bill's eyes were still open when they put him on the table. His legs oozed blood. She cut off the rest of his pants, and the damage to his legs was on full display. It looked ghastly, as bad as anything she'd seen in Afghanistan.

"Pressure," she said. "Wrap it in heavy gauze, bandages. Pack it, keep pressure on it. It's all we can do."

"They aren't be coming again for a while," said Bill. "I don't think I'm going to last that long." His eyes were open, but his skin was pale. He had lost a lot of blood, undergone a lot of shock. It was amazing he was alive at all. He looked a decade older than this morning. Soot and burns covered his face.

Mary didn't answer, cleaning out his wounds while Mike and Teddy looked down the hall. They couldn't help.

She cleaned the wounds as best she could, and dressed one. Bill grunted as she applied pressure. The shock of the injury was wearing off, and he wouldn't be able to stay conscious much longer. She had to get him stable first.

"Miss Mary," he said, his voice faint.

"I need to finish this, Bill," she said. "I'm trying to get you stable."

"Please, listen to me," he said. She didn't look at him, continuing to work.

"I'm listening, Bill," she said. He grabbed her with a hand, pulling her close to his face, surprising strength for a man who was dying.

"No," he said. "I need you here."

"Bill—"

"Please," he said. "Could you do one thing for me?"

"Bill—"

"Could you tell my momma that her biscuits made it to Antarctica?" he asked.

"I—"

"It'll make her smile," he said, grinning. "Farthest they've ever gotten. New world record."

"Sure thing," she said. She went back to work, finishing the dressings on one leg, and then working on the other. She dressed the other wound, washing, wrapping it in layers of gauze and bandages. She did what she could.

"Alright, Bill," she said. She would check his vitals, get him a blood transfusion if possible, if Schuller hadn't sabotaged the supplies. His eyes were open, but not blinking. She checked his pulse.

Nothing. Bill was gone.

"God fucking damnit!" she screamed, grabbing her keyboard and smashing it against the edge of the desk, keys flying off of it as she smashed it down and down again, until it broke in two.

"Mary," said Mike.

She threw it. Mike turned his head and closed his eyes as the last few keys flew off of it.

"We have to focus," he said. "If we want to survive."

Her heavy breathing filled the room.

"How did we get here?" she asked.

"A slow descent," said Teddy, from the door. "With no one doing enough to stop it."

22

"So what do we know?" asked Mary.

They had moved Bill's body, wrapping him in Mary's parka for the time being. Teddy laid on the table. Mary was removing the piece of metal from his leg.

"We know that the helicopter was sabotaged," said Mike. "It exploded, killing the pilot, Beth, Jim, and Bill."

"I found a note in my bag when I went back inside," she said. "A warning about a bomb. Left by Helena. I saw her disappear around a corner when I came in. She was trying to warn us."

"And Alex saw Andrew outside," said Mary. "This will hurt." She pulled out the shard of metal, hoping it would come out in one piece. Mary found no other pieces, even if the gash in his leg looked horrific. Teddy grunted in pain, but stayed still.

"That's quite a tickle," he said, his teeth gritted.

"Andrew is the chemist," said Mike. "He probably made the bomb. Attached it to the helicopter when no one was looking. Under orders from Schuller."

"Why did he blow it up?" asked Teddy. "He's a goddamn scientist."

"His ride is over when he goes back," said Mary. "He's out of his depth now, has been for a while. And he knows it. He's desperate. He thinks he can find the particles, or whatever was down there, inside us."

"With what?" asked Mike. "His geology degree?"

"He's not all there anymore. The cold, the deaths, the stress—it's taken its toll on him."

"Okay, even then," said Teddy, wincing as Mary flushed out his wound. "Why kill people? Why attack the chopper?"

"Maybe he just meant to break it," said Mary. "Strand us here for a few more days, until the weather clears and they send another one. It would have given him more people to study."

Mary closed the wound, stitching it shut, and covering it with a bandage.

"You're lucky," said Mary.

"You don't have to tell me that," said Teddy, glancing over at Bill's covered body. "So what do we do?"

"There are three of us," said Mike. "And three of them. One of which might be sympathetic, might be on our side, but is too afraid to do anything overt."

"We don't know that," said Teddy. "We don't know who left that note. She had chance after chance to leave, and she chose to stay with him."

Mary remembered the look in Helena's eyes, when she apologized for staying. Mary knew she had left it. Where did her loyalty lie? And if she still followed Schuller's orders, did it make a difference?

"We need to talk to McMurdo," said Mike. "They'll send reinforcements."

"With the weather the way it is," said Teddy. "They won't be here for days. They won't send another chopper out just to lose it. No matter the situation."

"We still need to tell them," said Mary. "They're in the dark, probably have been for weeks. Schuller is the one who files updates to them. Have they heard about anything since I've gotten here? They didn't know about Bart and Jane. Schuller has been feeding them lies. They need to know what's happened."

"Can we afford to wait a few days?" asked Mike. "They're dangerous, Schuller and Andrew especially. They're willing to kill. They could be anywhere in camp. And Schuller—who knows what he wants to do? What he's planning?"

"He doesn't have a plan," said Teddy. "He's lost his fucking mind, trying to avoid bills that he can't afford. He kills enough bill collectors, someone will notice."

"I don't want to be a dead bill collector," said Mary.

"I'm not saying we go belly up," said Teddy. "I'm just saying I wouldn't call anything he's done a grand plan. You said it, he's desperate."

Mary thought to the look in his eyes when he asked her to stay with him, over and over again. We need you, he said. Nothing works without you. But what could she do? Stitch up wounds and bury the dead.

"We have to talk to McMurdo," said Mary. "I think we

can agree on that. The radio room is at the far end of this building."

"And any of them could be hiding anywhere, with a knife, a club," said Mike. "And then we're done."

"I still don't think he wants to kill us," said Mary. "He needs us. He thinks those particles are inside. He doesn't want dead subjects. He wants live ones."

"Could have fooled me," said Teddy. "Fucking murderers, is what they are."

"We don't go anywhere alone," said Mike. "Strength in numbers. If we find Helena alone, we can try and talk to her, maybe she'll join us, given the chance, having seen what Schuller can do. Schuller, and Andrew—"

"They better hope I don't see them first," said Teddy. "What weapons do we have?"

"We have scalpels," said Mary. "There are tools in the garage, but that might as well be on Jupiter."

"There are knives in the kitchen," said Mike. "And steel trays that we can use as weapons or shields, if need be."

"So the kitchen, and the radio room," said Mary. "And we stick together. How's your leg?"

Teddy was standing now, testing how much weight he could put on the leg. He took a step, moving fast for the amount of damage done. The metal tore right through his muscle. He should barely be able to stand.

"It hurts," he said. "But it works. I can keep up."

"Can it hold your weight?" asked Mary. Teddy showed her by standing alone on the injured leg. He didn't try and hop up and down, but that alone was amazing.

"That should be impossible," said Mary. "Whatever that particle did to you—"

"I'll take it for now," said Teddy. "If it means I can walk."

"Let's prepare the bodies," she said. "And then we can get to work."

They braved the cold again, the wind blowing hard, un-relenting fury threatening to knock them off their feet, visibility decreasing by the moment. They had ran out of room inside, and they couldn't risk moving the bodies through the buildings when Schuller's group could be waiting anywhere with a club. They would stack them outside, in the cold. They afforded the dead all the respect they could.

Mary and Mike left Teddy inside, watching and listening. They carried Bill's body outside and then worked through the wreckage. The cold had wiped out the fires. Only a ball of blackened and burnt metal remained. The wind had carried away any stray debris, leaving only the largest pieces of metal strewn around the remains of the chopper.

They cut through what was left of the restraints for Jim and Beth. They pulled their bodies out, each on one side as the wind cut through them. Mary felt none of the cold, moving through it. Mike suffered. They put Jim's body next to Bill's, and then Beth's.

They struggled to pull out Alex's body from the cockpit. The metal had warped there, and they used a pry bar to wrench the door open, pulling out her scorched body, putting it with the others. Then they went to get Bart and Jane, who were still in the rear compartment.

The fire had been worse there, the explosion terrible, that close to the bomb and fuel tank. There wasn't much left recognizable of the bodies, but Mike and Mary put them with the rest, just the same. It felt right to keep them together. A toll of the blood on Schuller's hands.

On her second night in Afghanistan, before her first patrol, they had brought back a whole squad. Twelve men who all died to a a cleverly placed IED. They retrieved the bodies, and laid them out so they could be identified and taken care of properly. She had seen the true effects of the war they waged for the first time. As a combat medic, she had to fight to not be disillusioned, to not lose focus of the importance of every person's life, to try to keep fighting for every single soldier in her care. When presented with death and mutilation every day, desensitization is the only way to survive mentally. Caring too much is dangerous because your mind will break. She underwent dozens of check-ups, just to make sure the accrued mental toll hadn't broken her. She passed every one.

But it didn't mean she didn't struggle. She saw those twelve soldiers, and tried to remember they each had a family, each an entire life, a web of experiences that connected to thousands of people. They could not become numbers, even if she didn't know their names. They were still under her care, so she would have to remember them.

Those twelve she saw her second night would grow. Sometimes just one, or a half dozen, or entire groups of soldiers killed. Sometimes they died in front of her, but mostly they died in the abstract, a number of soldiers who walked out of base and then returned in a body bag, without a face.

She felt proud of her service. She had saved lives. Those interconnected webs of relationships, of ties, of importance—she kept them intact. Her actions had a definable impact. She never let fear conquer her. She had never let those soldiers become numbers. She endured that sorrow and horror and kept them in her mind as people. Each as the center of their own web. Important, valuable, *human*.

They laid out all the bodies in a row on the ice, the wind whipping past them. She knew the cold was there, but she didn't feel it.

She had spent time with all of them, drank with them, ate with them, and worked with them. Even with Alex, the pilot, she had spent more time than with most of the men who died in combat. She never knew most of those soldiers. The people in front of her—she knew their names and the faces. She had swapped stories and laughter with them.

She felt nothing. No sorrow. No pain. No horror. A simmering anger burned there, for Schuller, Andrew. But it was only because they tried to kill her. But she felt no anger, no sorrow about these people. When had it gone? She tried to save Bill, she did, but why? Why did she help Teddy? Why did she run out to the chopper, shouting? She could be experiencing shock, post traumatic stress disorder, her body cutting off emotional ties to prevent worse mental impact.

But she didn't think that's what it was. Her gut said otherwise.

Bart, before he killed himself, said that the other thing inside him had taken up more and more real estate, and he couldn't find himself anymore. She hadn't understood what he meant. Not really. The hallucinations and the visions were in full effect by then, but she still felt like her. She saw Bart open up his own throat and she felt indescribable terror as she watched him bleed out in front of her.

She understood now. She had no voice inside, no demon on her shoulder telling her to kill.

But the particle had stripped away her humanity. It had been pulled out like bad insulation and tossed into the wind.

Vestigial, obsolete.

Because she wasn't human anymore.

23

They needed weapons and they needed the radio.

Mary carried a scalpel, the metal blade wrapped with tape for easier handling. Mike carried his small pocket knife. Teddy held a spare board from the storeroom, pried off a crate, with a nail in the end. He limped as he followed them.

They worked their way through the main building, slowly, methodically, room to room, checking every space for a possible ambush. They would get to the radio room, find the things they needed, and then call for help.

They found nothing in any of the bunks, even Andrew and Helena's. They had cleaned theirs out with the rest, even though they stayed. They checked the rooms anyway, all three of them close together. They left doors open as they swept, against regulations. The cold was not the worst of their enemies, not anymore.

"Dollars to donuts they're all shacked up in Schuller's lab," said Teddy. "I'd bet my life on it."

"We don't know that," said Mike. "We can't assume anything. That's what led us here."

They found nothing else.

The building was quiet, with no footsteps or no echoes. Mary heard nothing as they moved through the building. Even with only a few people, any noise inside could be heard. The wind screamed outside, buffeting the building. The building stood.

They walked down the hallway, their weapons ready. No one came, and there was no sound. They found their way to the kitchen and mess hall, the largest room in the main building. No one waited for them there, the stainless steel spotless.

"I told you," said Teddy. "They're in Schuller's lab."

"I hope you're right," said Mike. "Let's see what we can get in here."

The knives had been cleaned and put away. Both Mike and Mary grabbed a chef's knife, six inch blades. Bill had kept them sharp, and they would cut through flesh like butter. Teddy snagged a tray, heavy and reliable, usable as a shield or as a weapon. The kitchen had been emptied of food. The storage rooms held all that remained.

They went there next. Schuller had taken the supplies.

They had pulled open crates, and upended boxes. Anything with food or water had been ripped apart, the contents taken from them.

"They took everything," said Mary.

"Should have guessed it," said Teddy. "He wanted it all for them."

"We were busy packing up," said Mike. "Didn't notice it."

"He wants us to come to him," said Mary. "We can't turtle up and wait. We have to go to him."

"He's lost his fucking mind," said Mike, picking through the remains of a box. It was full of cans, holes punched into them. "He doesn't want us to eat anything he left behind."

"What's that smell?" asked Teddy.

"Bleach," said Mary. "He covered anything left in bleach. Scorched earth."

"Jesus," said Mike.

"He's not here," said Teddy. "Remember what Schuller said? That we'd find God down in the ice? Whatever we found, it wasn't God."

Mary thought otherwise. Teddy walked firmly, less than an hour after she pulled a five inch piece of metal out of his calf. She'd have bet her life savings that if she peeled off his bandages, there'd be a healed wound underneath. The particles had given him incredible recuperative powers. Enough to fix a crippling wound in an hour. She would qualify that as a miracle. If a man of God performed it, they would be sainted.

Does Schuller know about Teddy? About her?

He had asked her. He knew.

They moved on from the storerooms. They checked the two science labs next, and then some utility spaces and the radio room. Still no sign of the traitors.

"Don't drop your guard," said Mike.

Schuller had emptied the labs of everything, including the equipment. The tables remained, but they had taken everything else.

"When did they do all this?" asked Mary.

"While you were trying to keep people alive," said Mike, plain. "Safeguarding their research. Schuller thinks they want to take it from him, probably moved everything to his personal lab."

"That's why he blew the chopper," said Teddy. "He didn't want anyone taking his work."

She had met Jim here.

She had pulled his corpse out of the helicopter, killed by Schuller's bomb. She felt a tinge then, something pulling at the corners of her, tugging at her heart. Sorrow. And then it vanished, replaced by the rage, the selfish anger. But she had felt it, if only for a moment.

"Teddy's right," said Mike. "I don't think they're here. Wouldn't be surprised if they barricaded themselves in Schuller's lab, with all the supplies, waiting for us to come knocking on their door."

"I'll come knocking on their fucking door," said Teddy. "I'll drive a goddamn tractor right through his entire building. Or turn off the power to it. Freeze them out. They'll come crawling out, and then we'll have them."

"We finish here first," said Mary. "We radio back, then we can worry about Schuller."

The utility spaces were left alone, filled with a few extra sets of blankets, bedding, cooking implements.

Only the radio room left.

They moved slower now, the three of them listening, hearing only the wind beating the walls of the building. Mary ducked her head into the room and checked the corners quickly. She held the chef's knife tight, ready to tilt it out across a neck of someone attacking her from a corner or behind the door.

No one waited inside, but the room was a mess. They went in.

"What the fuck happened in here?" asked Teddy.

Small tables were overturned, with notebook paper and chairs knocked over.

"There's blood," said Mike.

There was. Splashes and streaks of red stained the white linoleum floor, small pools here and there, and then smudged, with shoe prints etched in the blood.

"This was recent," said Mary, the blood still wet in spots. "Less than an hour."

"We would have heard it," said Mike.

"Would we?" asked Mary. "With the wind, with trying to keep Bill alive?"

"Then what happened?" asked Teddy. "Whose blood is this?"

"Helena's," said Mary.

"That was fast," said Mike.

"Schuller realized that she had tipped us off," said Mary. "Or she saw the true scope of what has happened to him. Realized that there was no coming back from where he's gone. Tried to pull him back, and he resisted."

"There's no body," said Mike. "She's still alive."

"We don't know that," said Teddy. "We don't know anything. They could have killed her and taken the body with them."

"Either way, they're not here," said Mike. "And the radio is. We can call McMurdo. Who knows how to work this thing?"

"I can do it," said Teddy. "A kid can practically operate these things nowadays, they're so fucking simple."

The radio sat on a side table, a large box with a few dials, a power switch, a few others. Teddy flipped on the power, and the radio hummed to life.

"That's strange," he said, leaning in to get a better look at one of the dials. He flicked it a few times. "That shouldn't be—"

The radio exploded, a massive blast filling the small room. The explosion threw Mary backwards, her ears ringing, her face wet with blood. Her ribs rang out with pain as she hit the edge of an upended table.

A goddamn trap. They fucking rigged the radio too.

She groaned, every breath filled with ragged pain. Broken ribs. She felt over to her side, and pushed with her fingers. She was met with an even stronger jolt. More than one was fractured.

She put her hands to her face, feeling the blood coursing down over her eyes, into her mouth. Her fingers probed, found a wound in her forehead. Not deep. Seemed to be the extent of the damage. Mike was rolling back and forth on the ground, holding his shoulder. She picked herself up and limped over to him.

"Mike," she said.

"Fuck," he said. "Think it broke my shoulder." The explosion had thrown him arm first into the wall. It looked lumpy and malformed, the wall dented where he hit it. Shoulders were complicated, and if it was anything but a straight dislocation, it'd be impossible to fix.

"Teddy," said Mike, and Mary heard him then, the ringing in her hears thinning. He groaned, alive, rolling on the ground.

Teddy cradled his face and moaned in pain, unintelligible noises coming out of him.

"Teddy," she said. "Can you hear me?"

He didn't stop moaning, his hands still on his face as he floundered. She grabbed his arm, trying to hold him still. His ears bled. He couldn't hear her. She grabbed his arms, holding them firmly, and pulled on them, with gentle pressure. She needed to see the damage to his face. He pulled his trembling hands away.

They revealed a bloody wreck. The blast had burned away much of the skin on his face, and sent pieces of metal from the radio casing into his flesh. He wore a crimson mask.

His eyes—oh God—his eyes.

They were ruined. The explosion had seared them in an instant, the fire scorching the soft sclera. He wouldn't see again.

Mike was on his feet, cradling his injured arm.

"Christ," he said, seeing Teddy's face.

"We have to get him back to my office," she said. "So I can try and help him."

"What about the radio?" asked Mike.

Mary looked at it, expecting little and getting less. They had rigged the trap to the power switch of the radio, and the explosion had destroyed most of it. Any thought to salvage it was thrown out the window when she saw the extent of the damage. They weren't engineers. The radio was gone.

She checked Teddy for any other injuries, and he was lucky in that regard. His face had taken all the damage. Her broken ribs screamed as she and Mike helped Teddy to his feet, holding him, trying to reassure him, deafened, blinded, as they moved him back to her office, back where they started.

She patched up Teddy's face as best she could, removing the micro-shrapnel, and stitching him up. His eyes were beyond her. Mary covered them with gauze and bandages. If they got back, maybe they could help him. She gave him a sedative for the pain and looked at Mike's shoulder.

The impact had torn a ligament in his shoulder, and damaged cartilage. That's all she could tell from the outside. She could only craft him a simple sling for his arm to rest in.

Her own ribs were surely broken. She would have to deal with the pain.

"What do we do?" asked Mike.

What were their choices? No radio, no supplies. Teddy blind and deaf, both her and Mike injured. They had some chef's knives.

"We kill them," said Mary.

24

"They're waiting for us," said Mike. "Attacking them is suicide. The first trap almost killed us. Schuller wants us to come to him. You said it yourself."

"What other choices do we have?" asked Mary. "Wait here and starve? Or until they attack us while we're sleeping? Who knows when the weather will allow for another helicopter? It could be a week."

"Teddy can't help," he said. "I have one arm."

"We don't have any other options," said Mary. "If we move fast, and surprise them, we have a chance."

Teddy was unconscious, the sedative putting him to sleep. He couldn't help them anyways. They'd have to leave him. Mike looked at her, a thousand thoughts passing over his eyes.

"What's the plan?" he asked.

"We use the cold," said Mary.

They moved through the main building again, staying together, leaving Teddy behind. They carried their knives at the ready. They headed for the garage.

They saw a few bare feet of ahead of them outside, bracing themselves against the wind, hands held tight to the lead line that ran between the buildings. The air roared past them. It hit them full force, nearly taking them off their feet.

The ever present cold did not penetrate Mary's skin. She resisted the urge to pull off layer after layer of clothing, to test her new self against the indefatigable cold, to truly test what she was now. The wind pushed her, but that's all it was. The cold had menaced her, but it was nothing to her anymore. They had opened up the ice. It had embraced her, accepted her, and shaped her to be one with it. She *was* the cold now, and she would use it to gain an advantage.

Mary and Mike held onto each other and the rope and found their way to the garage. They gathered themselves, ready for anything as they opened the door.

They heard nothing as they entered, the terrible wind left outside as they closed the door, the din pushed down and back. Mike did his best to shake off the cold in the garage. Mary felt nothing.

It looked undisturbed, the two tractors sitting on the concrete pad, with shelving and boxes everywhere. Bill had been their mechanic as well as the cook, and he worked on the tractors every night. Like the kitchen, he had left the garage in perfect shape.

They found hooks and chains and attached them to the outside of one of the big machines. Mike opened the garage

and got in the tractor, climbing up with one hand before settling in and starting the engine of the big machine. It roared
to life, and Mary climbed in next to him. The wind ripped
through the now open garage. They pulled away, around the
other buildings, next to Schuller's lab and living space. The
vehicle rocked as the air hit it.

Mary jumped out, grabbing the chains, leaning into the
wind to not get knocked over. The iron clinked in her hands,
and she pulled them, looking out for any interference from
either Schuller or Andrew. Despite the low visibility, neither
of them came out to stop her. She had halfway hoped they
would. She wrapped the chains around the wooden support
beams that attached the building to the foundation, hooking them around and pulling them taut.

They would rip the fucking wall off.

She scrambled back to the tractor.

"Gun it," she said. Mike gunned the accelerator, and
pulled them taut, letting the vast amounts of torque pull.
The engine whined as the chains started pulling on the
wooden supports. Mary looked back.

"Will the chains break?" asked Mary.

"They shouldn't," said Mike. "The tractor should shut
down before that will happen."

The wind howled by, and the tractor's engine strained as
it pulled. The tractor dug into the ice. The chains pulled at
the building's supports. The building was bolted down into
the ice, the only thing to mount it to. The ice wouldn't give.
The metal beams, the foundation, wouldn't give. But the
wooden supports would. They would flex, bend, and then
snap.

Neither Mike nor Mary heard the flexing, or the bend-ing, but they heard the snap, even over the horrendous wind. Two simultaneous gunshots rang out as thick wooden planks snapped, and without the support, the rest broke too. The tractor lurched forward, dragging the front wall of the building with them.

Mike killed the engine, and they looked back, the building's innards revealed to the cold. They grabbed their weapons and climbed down onto the ice.

The wind and haze hampered visibility, but Mary saw no one inside, no startled faces looking out into the cold. They each held their weapon out, ready for an attack.

No attack came. They entered the building, already cold, the bulwark against the ice and wind fallen. The lab section had been emptied, just like the main labs. The equipment remained.

No, Mary corrected herself, as she swept across the room again. She saw something else. A body, lying on a table in the middle of the room.

"Check his living quarters," said Mary. Mike skirted the edge of the room, his knife ready as he poked his head into Schuller's bedroom.

"No one in there," he said.

Mary acknowledged him, barely hearing him, her eyes focused on the body. It was Helena. What was left of her.

Mike came back to her, looking at the body, and then backed away, averting his eyes when he realized what he was seeing. Even after everything they had seen already.

She was bound, her arms and legs strapped to the table, naked. She had a long incision down the middle of her chest, her torso pulled open, her sternum cracked and spread. There was blood everywhere, smeared all over her and around her, pools of it freezing in the cold near their feet.

"What did they do to her?" asked Mike, looking at Mary.

They had cut into more than her torso. Her brain lay bare, the top of her skull gone.

"They opened her up," said Mary.

"What do you mean, they opened her up?" asked Mike.

"They cut her open," said Mary. "They dissected her. Schuller thinks the particles are inside us."

"So they cut her apart?" asked Mike. "They're geologists, chemists. What do they know about cutting people open?"

"Not much," said Mary, examining the incisions. They were clumsy. No doctor would cut like this. "It was a hack job. A first year medical student could do better."

Helena's head looked like it had been hit with an axe, to crack the skull open, and pried apart with pliers. Mary looked into the brain pan. Something seemed wrong.

"It explains why they didn't leave her body in the radio room," said Mike. "They wanted to look inside her. They needed the body. But why did they tie her down?"

Mary saw it, right away. Didn't think it needed explaining, but maybe she just knew how far Schuller had fallen.

"She was alive," said Mary. "When they started."

"No," said Mike. "No no no. What the fuck is happening?!?"

"This is where he is," said Mary. "He needs to see whatever it is he's looking for, and he will do anything to get it."

"Jesus fuck," said Mike.

Mary looked into the open torso again. She saw the same evidence.

"Can you shine a light?" asked Mary.

"You want to look inside of her?" asked Mike. "Why?"

"Just humor me," said Mary. Mike grabbed a penlight off his belt and shone it into Helena's open body, averting his eyes. Mary poked a gloved hand inside.

"What are you looking for?" asked Mike.

"Just trying to confirm something," said Mary, pulling her hands out.

"Trying to confirm what?" asked Mike.

"There are parts missing," said Mary. "Her lungs, her kidney, her heart, her stomach. All gone. Parts of her brain as well."

"They took parts of her? What the fuck for?" asked Mike.

"I don't know," said Mary, backing away.

"And how the fuck are so calm?" asked Mike. "I know you've seen combat and everything, but we're well past that at this point."

Was she calm? Helena's body shocked her, but she prodded and poked it without thought, with no horror or disgust. Could Mary reach down inside herself and find it, if she looked hard enough? Was that still in her? Helena had betrayed them, sure, but she had been in over her head, and it had cost her. She had tried to reverse course, but it had been too late.

Mary tried to summon some sympathy from deep inside her. Tried to find the horror of a person ripped apart while still alive. Nothing there. The thing inside had extinguished all that. Maybe it would come back, like the visions had gone away.

She said none of that.

"We don't have the luxury of losing control," she said. "Schuller and Andrew are out there, and we don't know where. We need to move on, and keep looking."

She walked away from Helena's corpse, into Schuller's room. All of his personal belongings were still there, left behind. Books, framed pictures, a tablet. Everything in his life that when put together, created the image of him.

His bed was made. Mary ripped off the comforter, dragging it back into the lab. She threw it over Helena's body and gave her what little respect they could muster.

"We should return the tractor to the garage," said Mary. "We might need it later, and if we leave it out in the cold, it'll never start again."

They left, climbing into the vehicle again. It was still warm inside. Mike sat, shaking and shivering, the extended time in the cold getting to him. Mary looked at him, immune.

He noticed her, and she noticed the noticing.

"Remember what Bart said," said Mary. "Before he killed himself? About, not being able to find himself inside anymore?"

"Yeah," said Mike. "He kept talking about that bucket."

"It's happened to me," said Mary. "I'm having trouble—I'm having trouble finding me anymore. I looked at Helena, and it was all—just tissue. She was just a thing."

Mike put a shaking hand on her shoulder, squeezing it.

"We will get out of this," he said. "And we'll get back to the mainland, and they'll figure this all out. And you'll be you again. We can't give up now."

"I don't even feel the cold anymore," she said. "It's changed my body, whatever we found. Teddy too. What's happening to me?"

"Remember what you told Bart," he said. "They'll fix

you."

Bart hadn't believed her. She didn't believe her either, not anymore. The particle had become a part of her, inseparable. They couldn't just put her in a centrifuge and spin the particle out.

"Can we sit for a minute?" he asked. "So I can warm up."

"Sure," she said. They sat in the cabin, Mike's trembling slowing and then stopping, as his body temperature rose again.

"No hallucinations yet?" asked Mary.

"Nothing," said Mike. "I'm one of the lucky ones, I guess. They went to greener pastures."

"I don't think there was any rhyme or reason," said Mary. "Where do you think Schuller is holed up?"

"They could be anywhere," said Mike. "It's been a wild fucking goose chase, and I'm about tired of it. Where are the supplies? Where's all their research? We've been through the whole camp."

Where else was there?

"The dig site," said Mary.

"Fucking hell," said Mike. "Of course. But when?"

"They could have been shuttling things over for days," said Mary. "Let's go back. They're not there now."

Mike drove the tractor back over to the garage. He pulled it into the bay. The wind had knocked the garage into disarray, crates and cardboard boxes everywhere. They got out, and Mary closed the door, the noise slowly diminishing as the door shut it out. She heard a sound from behind her.

She turned to see Andrew crouched over Mike's unconscious body. She felt a sudden jolt of pain to the back of her head, and then nothing.

25

"I told you we needed you."

Mary woke up, tied to a folding chair, her head aching. Schuller held a pistol at arm's length pointed at her head.

"You're awake," said Schuller, smiling. "Good. I didn't want to harm you too badly."

She opened her eyes, and her vision swam, before focusing. The pain on the back of her head stayed, joining the ache in her side. They had dragged the two of them them back to the main labs, empty still, except for them, and the tables that filled the space. Schuller stood in front of her with the gun. She couldn't move to get it from him if she tried. She hadn't known Schuller had a gun, that there was a gun at Tau at all. Another secret of his.

Teddy laid behind Schuller, strapped to a lab table. He

remained unconscious from the sedative she had given him. His face, burnt from the explosion, already looked better. They had them outnumbered, three to two, and it was for nothing.

"Where's Mike?" she asked.

"Don't worry, he's close by," said Schuller, gesturing with the gun behind her. She cocked her head, her neck aching, and she saw him. They had gagged him and strapped him to a chair. A thin trickle of blood dripped down the side of his head. Andrew stood next to him, watching Schuller, his eyes focused on his leader.

"All that strength didn't help him," said Schuller. "Not anymore. He should have watched his words earlier. I could have made it easy on him."

"Fuck you," said Mary.

"That isn't very polite," said Schuller, waggling the gun. "And I will not take any more push back from you or Mr. Hale. I bowed to that pressure too many times during this project, and we all suffered from it." He gestured at Andrew, who held a scalpel to Mike's neck.

"You will speak to me calmly," he said. "Or Andrew will cut Mike's throat."

Mary bristled but said nothing. She strained against the ropes that bound her, but they were tight, and tied well.

"All of this could have been avoided," he said. "If people had just listened. If they had just stayed, to push us towards our goal. But they fled, like cowards."

"You killed them," said Mary. "Innocent people. They did nothing wrong."

"They turned their back on discovery," said Schuller. "There is no greater sin, Ms. Jensen. But you survived through Helena's intervention. Fortuitous. Although a little late for her. I'm not much of a surgeon, I'm afraid. Andrew either. She suffered unnecessarily. You could have saved her a lot of pain if you had cooperated from the beginning."

"You're a monster," said Mary.

"She did try and betray me, Ms. Jensen," said Schuller. "After saying she was with us until the end. Duplicitous. She's not alone in that matter, but most have paid the price for their betrayals. Helena's was just more messy than others."

"You butchered her," said Mary. "For nothing. For your own satisfaction."

"That is not true, Ms. Jensen," he said. "I think you would agree, more than anyone, that the elementary particles in question are a part of us now. How else will we study them? How else will we find them? When they were in the ice, we dug. They may no longer be in the ice, but we *will still dig*."

He paced now, fingers steepling on the pistol, running up against the cold metal of the handgun. But Mary saw something in his eyes. Doubt, somewhere in him.

"What did you do with her organs?" asked Mary. She already knew, but she wanted to know if he would say it.

"That's immaterial," he said. He wouldn't tell her. His cheeks burned red and he averted his eyes.

"You ate them."

He only stared at her, making eye contact, breaking it, his eyes flitting between her, the floor, Teddy's unconscious body, Andrew, the middle distance, pacing, fingers running up and down the etched cold steel of the pistol.

"It's not fair, Ms. Jensen," he said. "I'm the one who's sweat and bled over this project. I pulled it up from the ground, I acquired funding, I defended it from overzealous, cowardly academics, who called it a waste of time and resources. Me. Me! And who got blessed with the spark? A bunch of uneducated simpletons, who can run a drill, complain about leadership, and run when things get tough. Who waste the gift with suicide, or with ignorance, or with fear. And I get nothing, no reward for my sacrifice. Well no more, not again! I will not be passed over again. I will receive the blessing, by any means necessary."

He barked now, like a rapid dog, spittle flying with every word. The rage had overwhelmed him.

"Helena wasn't affected," said Mary. "So you're a cannibal. For nothing."

"She could have been hiding it!" he barked. "Like you were hiding it, Ms. Jensen. No matter how you tried to hide it, I could tell. I could see the difference in you."

"Bullshit," she said.

"You can deny it all you want," said Schuller. "But I can see the change in your eyes. The indifference. Because the blessing, it makes you more. It makes you more than just human, and I don't care how much you talk about empathy, a divide is born. Between you and me. You're not one of us anymore, Ms. Jensen. You've moved past humanity. They've done it to you. They've elevated you. How does it feel?"

Schuller's eyes were on her now, shining, gleaming. The pistol hung loosely by his side.

"I don't feel different at all," she said, avoiding his eyes.

"Don't lie to me, Ms. Jensen," he said. "This is for posterity's sake. We need to record all of this. Don't risk Mr. Hale's life over obstinacy."

Andrew stood next to Mike, a scalpel ready, waiting for

Schuller's order. His lone loyal soldier, still serving.

"I don't feel different at all," she said. Schuller stared at her, his gleaming eyes hardening. His nostrils flared.

"Kill him," said Schuller, still staring at her. "Cut his throat."

"Wait," she said, her voice loud in the lab. "I don't know who I am anymore."

"A loss of identity," he said. "So Bart wasn't an isolated case. What does it feel like? Losing yourself?"

"Bart was wrong," she said. "What was me isn't sloshing out of a bucket, spilling onto the ground. I wasn't forced out, by some alien invader. But I was replaced. I was overwritten. New data on top of mine."

"That's amazing," said Schuller, the gleam in his eyes returning. "You're becoming more."

"I wouldn't say that," said Mary. "I'm not more. I'm just other."

"You don't understand the gift you've been given," he said.

"I understand enough," she said.

"I'll have it," said Schuller. "Soon. Whatever it takes. Andrew, cut her loose."

Andrew left Mike's side, and moved behind Mary. The ropes that tied her slid free, and she could move again. Schuller raised the pistol again, pointing at her, the metal gleaming under the glow of the lights in the lab.

"Go next to Teddy," he said, gesturing with the handgun. Schuller stood five steps from her. Could she get to him, avoid his first shot, take the gun from him, and stop Andrew before he attacked her?

"Move," said Schuller, keeping his distance from her. Andrew moved back to Mike, the scalpel pressed to his neck.

She moved, walking over to Teddy's body, tied down to the lab table. She checked his pulse. Slow, but steady. Schuller hovered around her, a cone of light on her and Teddy.

"Cut off his shirt," said Schuller. Andrew handed her a pair of scissors, and she looked at him, hesitated, and then slid it underneath the dark cotton of Teddy's shirt and cut through, revealing his bare torso.

"I see that Teddy received the brunt of our trap," said Schuller. "I know he has the blessing. He was stronger, like you. Didn't succumb, like Bart. Take off the bandages around his eyes." Schuller's voice commanded from behind her, the dim lab beyond the bright lights above her. Without looking, she could feel Andrew next to Mike, the razor sharp blade pressed against his throat. She peeled off the layers of bandage and gauze she had packed over his injuries just hours earlier.

The metal shrapnel had destroyed his eyes. Mary had assumed it was outside the reach of his newfound recuperative powers. An eye wasn't a leg. The eye is a complicated organ.

With the bandages removed, Mary could see that whatever had changed in Teddy wasn't trifling. It was groundbreaking.

His eyes had healed a startling amount in two hours. The superficial damage was gone, and as Mary pulled back his eyelids, his eyes were still damaged, but they worked, the pupils dilating with the light, the white no longer a chewed up mess or destroyed by fragments of metal. It was impossible.

"He's healing, isn't he?" asked Schuller.

"Yes," said Mary, staring.

"It's the blessing," said Schuller. "It's transforming him. Making him more than human. This is what they laughed at. He is the key to all of it. I should thank Helena. She made this possible."

"Made what possible?" asked Mary. Teddy stayed unconscious.

"Our mission hasn't changed, Ms. Jensen," he said. "We need to find the particles, wherever they may be. We know they are in Mr. Ramirez. They've already worked miracles inside of him. And they will allow all of us to share that blessing. It is a sign. A sign that I was right."

His voice was getting louder and louder. Schuller had one more sermon in him.

"Pick up the scalpel," said Schuller.

One sat next to Teddy, in a small surgical tray filled with various tools, the few they stocked at Tau. Enough for minor operations, nothing more.

She turned around, facing Schuller, who was pointing the pistol at her now, ten feet from her. The bore faced her, the black hole threatening death.

"I'm not cutting him," said Mary.

"You will," said Schuller. "Or Andrew will cut Mike's throat."

Andrew held the blade to Mike again. Andrew's eyes were manic, a slick grin sneering at her. Mike's eyes stared at her.

"We don't have any anesthetic," said Mary. "Nothing for something like this."

"We can't use an anesthetic," said Schuller. "It might spoil the blessing. You've already done too much, giving him the sedative. We need him alert, awake. Teddy is strong now, stronger than any of us. The spark has made him strong. Any damage we do will be repaired in short order. He is *infinite* now. It was their will."

"I won't," said Mary. "I can't."

"Then Mike dies," said Schuller. "It's your choice, Ms. Jensen. Operate on Teddy, and I'll spare your lives."

She looked to Mike, his eyes wide, the blade pressed to his throat, a thin bead of blood welling up, dripping down his neck. His eyes gave her no answer.

"Please, Ms. Jensen," said Schuller. "It's an easy choice. Teddy's body will heal any damage you do. He is superhuman now. Mike is just a man, and your close friend. No one liked Teddy anyway."

Mary turned away from Mike's eyes, and Andrew's blade, and Schuller's gun. She picked up the scalpel, the blank canvas of Teddy's torso in front of her, spotless and ready. Mary's hand stayed steady.

"Teddy holds what I need inside of him," said Schuller.

Schuller's voice got closer, louder, reverberating through the room, through her.

"Open him up. Take him apart. Find God in him. And I will let you live."

26

Mary hoped the sedative would keep Teddy under.

He woke up thirty seconds into the operation.

Her hand was steady as she slid the blade down his chest, cutting a Y, just like an autopsy.

"I want a piece of every major organ," said Schuller, the gun pointed at her, his voice booming. "The spark could be hiding anywhere. I will not let it pass me by again."

The scalpel slid through the skin with the only barest of force from Mary. Blood began to well as she cut, and she dabbed at it with a towel as she worked, absorbing as much as she could. It still spilled off his sides, turning what was left of his shirt dark red. When she joined the Y on his torso, the two incisions meeting, Teddy woke up. His eyes opened suddenly and his head craned up, trying to see his predicament. Mary's blade was cutting him. Her gaze met his.

He yelled into his gag, the words muffled. Mary froze. Her blade hovered over the wound.

"Why have you stopped?" Schuller asked.

"He's awake," said Mary.

"Good," said Schuller. "Continue."

Teddy struggled against his restraints, but couldn't loosen them. Andrew must have been a boy scout.

"I'm sorry," said Mary, and she continued cutting, even as Teddy's muffled screams washed over her. She could feel Schuller's gun pointed at her. Would it be better to die, than to continue?

No. She must continue. Survive.

The scalpel traced down Teddy's torso, cutting through layers of skin and muscle, inches deep, below his belly button. He thrashed against his restraints. Mary's hand was steady. The blood spilled out of him, and she sopped up what she could. He would die soon.

She peeled back his flesh, revealing the ribs and breastbone, the intestines, stomach, internal organs all revealed. The pain would be indescribable, but Teddy remained conscious, his eyes staring at her, screaming at her, *screaming* at her.

"I told you we needed you, Ms. Jensen," he said. "So neat. So clean. Already much better work than I did on Helena. Cut me a piece of each organ. Each in the tray."

Teddy's eyes pleaded with her, and she ignored them. She must continue. She must survive. At any cost.

The stomach first. She held it in place, and sliced off a piece, the scalpel cutting through the soft flesh. Teddy shook, screamed into his gag. His skin turned pale as the blood oozed out of him.

The intestines next, small and large. Ropes piled into him, neat coils laid in line, row after row. She had heaped them back into dying men, putting them back into emptying cavities, reassuring men they would live, they would live, pressing their guts into them. She cut off a piece of one, and then the other, pain overwhelming Teddy's eyes, the muscles in his arms and legs taut as he pulled at his restraints, flopping back and forth like a dying fish. He would die soon.

Liver and kidneys. They were underneath, buried beneath the intestines, and Mary pushed them aside, piles of meat, moved out of the way, to the organs she needed. She would cut the pieces, she would do as she was asked. Survive. Don't think about the pain ripping through Teddy. He would die soon, then it would be over. *It won't be over, not until Schuller has the blessing or thinks he does. Not over until he consumes Teddy, and you, and Andrew, and Mike, and then each and every one of the corpses, picking through them, still eating them as they send a new chopper, and they hunt him down on the ice, ranting about the blessing, the spark, the elemental particles.*

Liver and kidneys. She found the liver, and cut a piece, and then did the same for the kidneys. Teddy wasn't here, wasn't alive. A dead body lined up, just like all the others. He would die soon.

She put the pieces in the tray, small pieces of flesh, shades of pink and red and purple, all there.

"Andrew," said Schuller. "Bring them to me."

Andrew left Mike's side. Mary turned. Schuller's eyes stayed on her, his gun pointed at her. Andrew walked up and grabbed the tray. Mary imagined grabbing him then, her blade to his throat, cutting him from ear to ear, his blood and Teddy's together, Andrew finally paying for his part in this.

But Schuller wouldn't care. He considered Andrew a drone. She knew it because they *all* were that to him. And killing Andrew then would kill her and Mike. Teddy would suffer for nothing. She would survive.

Andrew took the tray to Schuller.

"Hold it," said Schuller, still pointing his gun at Mary, took a piece from the tray, and laid it on his tongue, closing his mouth, chewing, swallowing. Then another. Piece by piece, gnashing through viscera and sinew, connective tissue and muscle, drips of blood and gore coating his mouth, his lips, his chin. By the last piece, it dripped off of him.

There was no science in this. Schuller only wanted the spark. From the beginning, Schuller had only wanted this, and now he would realize that want in its purest form. His mind contained no dissonance.

"I want the lungs and heart," he said, looking at Mary. "Reveal them. Give me them."

"He will die," said Mary.

"No, he won't," said Schuller. "The blessing keeps him alive. They persisted, and so will he. This is their offering to us. Continue to work. Our deal still stands. His pain is momentary."

Teddy stayed alive. The blood had stopped pouring out of him, and the color returned to his skin. His eyes danced in his head, but he wasn't dying. Schuller was right.

Mary had only the roughest ideas of how to get to his heart. She grabbed scissors from the tray, thick and heavy.

They shone under the lights. The ribcage shone too, and she would cut through it. The ribs connected to the breastbone which protected the lungs and heart. She would have to remove it. To Teddy, it would feel like she was ripping out his chest. Because she was.

The scissors sheared right through the thick cartilage that connected the breastbone to the ribcage. She worked her way up the ribcage, each rib snapping as she snipped through the cartilage. Teddy screamed every time. She finished his right side and then worked on his left. His body shook, but it didn't stop her. Her hands were steady. She would survive. He would die soon.

She finished cutting and pulled out his breast bone. She sliced open the thin tissue protecting the lungs and heart, the only thing left shielding them. There was nothing left stopping her. Teddy's eyes weren't looking at anything anymore, staring straight up. His thrashing had stopped. He had retreated inside.

"Give me them," said Schuller. She sliced a piece of lung, as they inflated and deflated in front of her. Teddy still breathed. She pushed it aside, and his heart was there, pumping hard, thumping in his chest, shaking with every pulse of blood, in and out, in and out. She cut a slice of flesh off it, and it bled.

She put them on the tray, his heart and lungs. Andrew grabbed it and took it to Schuller. Schuller ate them, first the lungs, then the heart. His jaw clicked as he bit through the chewy muscle. Mary looked at Teddy, Schuller's jaw clicking behind her. His chest opened, his sternum removed, his ribs broken, his organs excised. He still lived. He would die soon. He stayed conscious. The spark kept him alive. Any normal person would have passed out from the pain.

"Please stop this," said Mary, still looking at Teddy's glassy eyes. "This is inhuman." *Continue, survive.*

"You aren't human anymore, Ms. Jensen," said Schuller. "And neither is Teddy. And soon, I won't be either. And Teddy will heal. He can withstand anything. And we aren't done yet."

"What else is there?" asked Mary, but she already knew. She remembered Helena.

"The seat of the soul, Ms. Jensen," he said. "The pineal gland, hidden deep in the brain. Because I suspect, if there's a place for the spark to exist, to inhabit, to thrive, it is there."

Mary shook her head, no, this is enough, she wouldn't be his butcher anymore, but then Andrew had his blade at Mike's throat again, sneering at her, Schuller's pistol pointed at her. He would die soon. She should finish her work. Mike watched her with angry eyes. They had made him helpless. Teddy had screams for his gag. Mike had nothing.

"Use the ice saw," said Schuller. "Open up his skull. Find his soul."

The saw was barely more than a dremel, used by Jim to cut through samples of ice brought back to the lab. She picked it up, feeling Helena's blood wet beneath her fingers. Contamination was the least of her worries.

She had only the barest of ideas of how to cut through a skull. If there was head trauma in combat, a soldier's chances of survival were at the bare minimum to begin with. Teddy's eyes looked up at her, pleading for help. Whatever fugue state he had entered, he had returned to his mind.

"I can't do this," said Mary.

"You will," said Schuller. "Or Mike will suffer worse than

Teddy before he dies."

"This will kill him," said Mary.

"They persist, and so will he," said Schuller. "Do your work, and you will live."

She looked into Teddy's eyes, and then brought the saw down onto the middle of his forehead, the skin ripping where the saw touched, the small rotary saw whining as it bit into the bone. Blood trickled down the sides of his face as she worked. The dremel made its way through the skull, and she began to work around. Teddy screamed and screamed, as Mary took off the top of his head, working through the bone, circling the skull. She propped up his head, as she circled around the back of it, minutes passing, the dremel whining, the scent of singed flesh turning her stomach. Somewhere inside of her, there were indelible parts that were still human. Or maybe the smell was so instinctual, even her new self couldn't help it.

And then she was done, and like an obscene cartoon, she pulled off the top of his skull. Mary revealed his brain, a clean piece of bone covered in hair and skin in her hand. She put it aside.

"I don't know where the pineal gland is," she said, looking up at Schuller.

"Oh please," said Schuller, waggling his gun at her. "Don't try and fool me, Ms. Jensen."

"I'm a goddamn medic," said Mary. "Not a brain surgeon. I don't know what the fuck you expect from me, but finding a piece of the brain I've never even heard of before is not something I can do."

Schuller's eyes narrowed.

"Andrew," he said. Andrew left Mike's side. Schuller

handed the gun to him. "Monitor her. Move away, Ms. Jensen."

She did, palming a scalpel as she did so. This was her chance.

"I will do it. Even with my rudimentary knowledge, I think I can find it," he said. He grabbed a scalpel from the tray, and began to cut through the brain tissue. She knew there were no nerves in the brain, so Teddy felt nothing, even as his primary motor functions were damaged, his mind being sliced through, digging. She stood by, Andrew pointing the gun at her, staring at her. Schuller worked, his hands covered in blood. Like Mary's.

He grunted in frustration.

"I can't see a thing," he said. "Andrew, give me light."

Andrew looked at her, looked away, grabbed the small pen light in the tray, and moved where he could give Schuller light and keep an eye on her. His eyes flicked between the two, the gun pointed at her still. Back and forth between the two. She would only have a moment. She held the scalpel tight, and then as his eyes flicked down, she tossed it towards Mike. If it bounced off his lap, they were done for. The two would hear it and see the subterfuge.

It landed without a sound in his lap, and she looked back at Andrew just as his eyes flicked back toward her. He didn't betray seeing anything, and she stood still, her eyes downcast, as Schuller dug inside Teddy's mind. Teddy's eyes still looked at her. Pleading, tears rolling down his cheeks, mixing with the blood. She saw it now. Not pleading for them to stop. Pleading for her to kill him.

Mary could reach Teddy's open chest cavity. She saw his heart and lungs. She snuck a glance at Mike, the scalpel gone from his lap, his hands working while no one watched him. Andrew focused only on helping Schuller as he cut into Teddy's brain. She grabbed the scissors from the table and snipped through the carotid and pulmonary artery connected to his heart. Teddy's eyes looked at her, grimacing, but at peace. He would die soon.

The damage was too much, even for what Teddy was now, and blood poured out of the arteries, filling his chest cavity. Schuller still cut through his brain, pulling pieces out, trying to get to the pineal gland, buried deep inside. Mary watched as Teddy died. Andrew noticed before Schuller did.

"I think he's dead, Doctor," said Andrew, the first words he'd uttered since she came to.

"That's impossible," said Schuller. "They persist."

"He has no pulse. His chest cavity is full of blood," said Andrew.

"They persist, they persist!" he yelled, pushing Andrew out of the way, looking inside of Teddy. His eyes then went to her.

"What did you do?" he asked.

"I ended this savagery," she said. "They didn't persist. They couldn't withstand a pair of scissors."

A look of utter rage passed over Schuller's face, a thundercloud passing overhead, and then he was normal again, staring at her, his eyes narrowed.

"That was a mistake, Ms. Jensen," he said. "We had a deal, but you had to break it. And we need a replacement subject, without Mr. Ramirez. You will have to suffice. I doubt you'll withstand the punishment he did, but we will find out. Andrew."

Andrew advanced on her, gun out, pointed at her, Schuller behind him, his hands still bloody, holding the same scalpel he used on Teddy.

"Don't damage her, Andrew," he said. "We need her in one piece."

They advanced, and then Mike hit Andrew with full force, knocking him off his feet, launching him into the air and spearing him into the ground. Something cracked in Andrew, and the gun flew out of his hand, pinwheeling in the air.

Everything happened fast. Mike was on top of Andrew, choking him as Andrew struggled. Schuller ignored them both, diving after the pistol. Mary did the same. They grappled with each other, both going after the weapon, their hands wet with blood, slipping off of each other.

Mary grabbed him by the collar and elbowed him in the face, but Schuller took the blow even as his nose broke, and kneed her in her broken ribs, and Mary couldn't breathe. He scrambled to his feet, his nose already bleeding, trying to pick up the gun from the ground, the metal slipping between his wet hands. Mary inhaled a fresh breath and ignored the pain in her side, scrambling on her hands and knees over the bloody floor, grabbing a hold of his wrist, pulling him away from the gun. They struggled for a tight second before Schuller kicked her in the side, once, twice, the pain ripping through her, and she let go of the gun.

Schuller grabbed it and ran, firing three shots in quick succession before turning and running out into the hallway. BANG BANG BANG. Mary felt a shot whiz past her ear, a thin tunnel of wind carved near her head. She reached to her ear and felt blood, the bullet grazing her. She looked back.

Mike and Andrew were on the ground, both on their backs, next to each other. Andrew was dead. Mike clutched his chest. He was hit. She ran to him.

"Let me look at you," she said, pulling away his hand. Blood poured out of him. The bullet had hit him square in the chest. She could hear the whistle as he breathed. It had hit a lung.

"At least this will be easier than Teddy," said Mike.

"You're not dying here," she said.

"I don't have any magic in my pocket like you," he said. "It's okay. I did my best."

"Let me get you on a table," she said. "I've seen worse."

"There's no help coming soon," he said. "I'm a dead man. It's okay. Made my peace when the helicopter blew. Just stay with me."

She looked at him, met his gaze.

"We were good. Right?" he asked her.

"Yeah," she said. "We were."

"Sorry I fucked it up," he said. "Could have been something."

"Don't—" she started. He waved her off.

"Get out of here," he said. "Promise me."

"I promise," she said.

"Kill that motherfucker," he said. "And get out of here. Don't die—in the cold." His breath was shorter now, and within a minute, he couldn't breathe at all.

She held him and he died.

27

Mary walked across the ice through the wind and snow after Schuller. Steam enveloped her. He drove to the dig site, and she followed.

She had no tears for Mike, but she covered his body. Mary did the same for Teddy, taking the time to put him back together, giving back what little humanity she could to him. She covered him as well. She didn't wash her hands. She left them stained with blood.

Mike had strangled Andrew. She left his corpse. She had no empathy or sympathy for him. Whether by the cold, by Tau, by Schuller, by the sparks themselves, all of her mercy and pity had been erased.

She swept the building, but Schuller had fled, a trail of half-bloody footprints leading down the hall, leading to a door to the outside. She followed it, already knowing where he would flee. Schuller had taken everything to the dig site. Nothing remained in Tau for Schuller. Except for her.

She opened the door and a maelstrom hit her. The wind had picked up, almost knocking her off her feet. It roared past her ears, and she closed the door behind her. The wind had kicked up any snow on the ground and dropped visibility to nothing. She could barely see her hands in front of her face. She grabbed the guide line, moving by touch, going to the garage. She didn't feel cold without her outer parka, even as the wind whipped straight through her.

Schuller had left the garage doors open, with everything in the building without weight tossed around and pulled outside. Schuller had taken one of the tractors. She smelled the smoke from the other, even before she examined it. Smoke poured from the cabin. Schuller had dumped a container of diesel fuel inside, lit it on fire, and then thrown another in for good measure. He had destroyed the interior, along with all the controls. There was no way to the dig site now. Even in good weather, the tractor would be chancy, but without it, it was impossible.

No. Not for her.

The cold didn't affect her, and it was only far by Antarctic standards, where a hundred feet could mean death outside. It was just over two miles to the site. She would follow him, and she would kill him.

As the permanent midnight of winter came closer and closer, the days had gotten shorter and shorter. Only the tracks left by the rolling treads of the tractor guided her, with the sun down, and visibility nil. The wind and snow roared past her vision. If she got lost, it didn't matter if the cold wouldn't kill her. She'd starve, wandering on the ice.

She couldn't stay there.

She followed.

Mary flipped on the flashlight she grabbed from the garage, a long, four D-battery bastard. The strong light cut through the wind and snow, illuminating the tread tracks in front of her. She pointed it down at the tracks and started, her feet tracing them.

She walked, the wind howling, the snow blowing by her face. She could feel it hit her skin, and stick, and then melt, drops of water flowing down her face like tears. Her collar soaked through after a few minutes.

It should kill her, wet clothes here. Any liquid should flash freeze. But it didn't. She wouldn't allow it.

She felt the cold, like before, felt the stark alien cold, surrounding her, blowing past and through her.

No, not through. She felt comfortable as she walked in the dark, the light shining on the ice in front of her, the tracks frozen into the snow. She was protected, just like the sparks had been, so far down, in the dark, in the cold, in the crushing ice. They had protected themselves, put themselves into stasis to survive, in the coldest place on Earth.

And they did the same for her.

She followed.

She had never killed anyone, even in Afghanistan.

But she had watched men die.

Mary had been with a squad, cave hunting for the Taliban. Their APC had been disabled with an IED, and they had lost their engineer. They had been stranded.

Their commander took it as a sign they were close, and he was right. They found a local cell in a cave, and there was a firefight. They cleaned out the cell, but only Mary and two others survived. One of them had a bullet in his leg.

They carried him back to the APC, but they found more insurgents there, searching for them. Six of them.

They were outnumbered, and one of them was injured.

So they set a trap.

They laid down the injured soldier, and when the insurgents found him, they opened fire. The insurgents had no cover, and were mowed down quickly. But not by Mary.

She had fired, but she had missed every shot. She couldn't do it, couldn't shoot them. She knew they were dangerous, and wouldn't hesitate to do the same to her. But she couldn't do it.

They were still human. Still people. She didn't know what path they took that had led them there. To warring against America. But they were still human.

And so she fired, and she missed. It didn't matter. They were flat footed and out in the open and the other soldier killed them all, firing quick bursts into their chests.

The last one alive had thrown down his gun and shouted "surrender, surrender", his arms in the air. He fell to his knees, and begged for mercy.

The other soldier had advanced, and Mary followed.

They were close to the insurgent, and he looked up at them, his eyes wide open, tears flowing down his face. He begged for mercy. His eyes caught hers, and he saw her mercy, and he begged even more.

And then the soldier shot him in the chest, and he died.

It had left her breathless. Even after all that death and slaughter. It was different. She had fought to keep that humanity. To protect life at all costs.

She couldn't find it anymore.

The wind howled around her, circling her. She walked, without a measure of distance. The memory of marching through the desert echoed as she walked.

She wasn't human anymore. She had buried the thought, pushed it around her head, tried to find a place for it to stay, but she found no home for it, and now it sat in the middle of her mind, unavoidable. She felt alien to herself. Her emotions gone or muted.

Schuller had killed Mike and did she feel anything about it besides the rage, the anger at Schuller? Was her empathy gone forever? Was this where she belonged now, in this wasteland? The spark had shaped her for it. No cold could kill her.

She reached inside, tried to find sadness about Mike's death. She found something, a momentary vestigial twinge of pain, and it kept her walking. She would be driven by more than vengeance. That sadness would be the anchor point for her humanity, however much it eroded. Adrift in the void inside her mind, a small planetoid that she would grab onto, hold, and not let go.

She looked down and saw no tracks.

No, she had lost them, lost them while she was lost inside herself. The spark hadn't driven out her sense of panic. Survival was tantamount, and panic was evolution. Her heart started racing, and she tried to control her breathing.

Stop, first stop, she needed to stop, retrace her steps, return to the path, but they had vanished, blown away by the wind, and she could feel the panic, and she ran back, back to where she was, where she thought she was, she needed to find the tracks, she couldn't see, the damned wind, the storm, the snow, the ice, the cold, if she was so damned evolved why couldn't she see ten feet in front of her god-damned face and then she could.

Mary stopped. She saw now. The wind howled around her, but farther away. A sphere of peace circled her, her own eye of the storm. She spun her light around, and she could see twenty feet around her. The wind and snow only existed outside of the bubble surrounding her. She was doing this. The spark hadn't given her warmth. It had given her control.

Mary couldn't see the tracks. She had gone too far off course. The sphere of quiet was constant. She needed to see more. She tried something. She pushed.

The sphere widened in all directions, to thirty, forty, fifty feet. The flashlight cut through the darkness, shining off the ice beneath her. She saw the tracks in the distance, as she swept the area with her flashlight. They were still there, still dug into the ice. They would be until the ice melted, until the Earth warmed and killed them all.

She followed the tracks to Schuller, the cold, the wind, the snow held away from her.

She found the dig site.

She found Schuller.

28

Mary heard the drill before she saw Schuller.

One flood lamp illuminated the drill, its motor running, the nearby generators humming. As she approached, her calm surrounded the drill, removed the storm from it, and its loud churning could be heard, now, in the bubble.

Schuller worked, covered in layers, dashing back and forth. He didn't notice her. She didn't see the pistol, but she wasn't afraid of it anymore.

"Didn't know you knew how to work that thing," she yelled, over the din of the machine. Schuller turned his head, staring at her, stunned.

"You—" he said.

"Me," she said. "Turn off the drill, Doctor."

He hit the power button. The machine slowed, whirring

down to no sound at all. The generators hummed quietly behind her. He stared at her saying nothing, and as the machine spun down, the noise vanished. They stood in the silence.

"They're not down there anymore," said Mary. "Don't know why you're still looking."

"You're doing this?" asked Schuller, uncovering his face, pulling back the goggles and the scarf.

"Yes," she said. "You talked about a blessing. This is mine."

"Remarkable," he said. Schuller pulled off his gloves and drew the pistol out of his coat pocket. He pointed it at her. "You shouldn't have followed me, Ms. Jensen."

"What are you doing?" she asked. She stared at him, a lone figure, bundled against the cold. He looked so small.

"You will help me," he said. "We will find the spark in you."

"You're not going to shoot me, Doctor," she said. "I'm all that's left of your discovery. Shoot me, and it's gone forever."

"No," he said. "We'll find more. We know what to look for now."

She laughed. She laughed loud, and hard, a smile cracking her face for the first time in days. Schuller's nostrils flared, his eyes widened.

"Don't laugh at me!" he yelled, his voice cracking.

"Do you hear yourself?" she asked. "We know what to look for now. Who's we, doctor? Got a mouse in your pocket? You're alone. You always have been. From the moment I've been here, there has been one constant, that you are alone. Alone in your belief. Alone in your obsession. Alone."

"Andrew," he said. "Helena, my team. They believed in

me. We showed them—"

"Showed who?" she asked, walking closer to him. "Who are these invisible boogeymen who talk about, over and over and over? The academics? The doubters? The ones you lump all of your problems on? So many doubters in your life, Dr. Schuller. So many people who you dislike, or even seem to hate. The commonality about all of those people isn't them. It's *you*."

He lowered the gun now, slowly, his eyes unable to look at her anymore.

"You're the problem," said Mary. "You were never wrong. About the importance of what we were going after, about the sparks, the blessing. You were right, about everything. But you fucked it up. The greatest scientific discovery of our time will be known as a colossal disaster, a tragedy. Eleven dead, and all that science squandered."

He raised up the pistol, staring at her, his eyes narrowed in anger.

"No!" he yelled.

"I can freeze your hand solid, Doctor," said Mary. "And your pain means nothing to me."

She didn't know if she could, but she thought she could. She was immense.

His anger didn't disappear, but he lowered the gun.

"Drop it," she said, and he did, the metal clanking as it hit the ice.

"Are you happy now?" he asked.

"No," she said. "Not yet. Why did you kill Steve?"

She hadn't forgotten the forged psyche eval. She wanted all his debt to be known before the end. Schuller looked away from her, his face twitching.

"He found out I forged my psyche evaluation. He was going to tell McMurdo. They would have pulled me. It would have killed the mission. I could not allow it."

"No," said Mary. "I think the mission would have been fine. Helena could have led it. Or Jim. Even Andrew. But it had to be you."

"It was my mission! Mine. And you took it from me!"

He cried as snot dripped from his nose.

"I was supposed to find the particles. And I was supposed to receive the blessing. And I was supposed to go back to the world as a champion. And you took it all away from me."

"You never had anything," she said. "It was never yours to begin with. Who did the sparks go to? Me, Teddy, Bart, maybe someone else. We'll never know, because you killed them all. You don't see it?"

Schuller said nothing, tears running down his face.

"I understand now," said Mary. "I understand why Bart lost it. It's a lot to handle. I remember what you said, about these particles being the deciding factor in the evolution of man. Between us living and dying. I've struggled myself, with the changes. Change is hard for the best of people. But look at yourself. You couldn't handle any of this. Why would they choose you? What's so special about you?"

The generators hummed, and the wind howled outside her bubble.

"You're nothing," she said. "You think you can just keep drilling and stumble upon more? You squandered every opportunity you've been given, which has been many, and all you do is blame others. You've never confronted *you*. You've never looked inward, and it's cost eleven people their lives. So much pain, so much death. For what? For you?"

"How—" he started, but she cut him off.

"No," she said. "No more preaching. No more chapel. All the dead get no more words, and neither will you. You will do what I say. Pull up the drill."

He looked at her with menace in his eyes. She didn't warn him, only brought the calm inward, and the storm, the stinging wind and ice enveloped him. She felt it there, out there, floating. She made it worse, temperatures lower than ever recorded on Earth. Long enough for him to feel it. He screamed.

She pushed it back, the calm around him again. He shook, covered in snow already beginning to melt.

"Pull up the drill," she said. The menace in his eyes was gone. She had beaten him, and it felt good. He did as she said, the motor powering up to a loud roar. He held the lever, and the winch pulled the drill head up, slowly, thousands of feet below, the borehole opened up again. It was deep and dark. She could feel it there, familiar.

They waited. The winch dragged up the line, the calm protecting them, the storm blowing harder than ever outside of it. She watched him, his eyes staring sullenly at the ground. He did what he was told.

The drill reached the surface, the winch slowing, then stopping.

"Move the drill out of the way," she said. Schuller complied without looking at her, swinging the arm, the drill gone. There was only the hole now, the dark circle that went deep into the ice. It had called to her earlier. Was it them, seeking her out?

It was an open grave, and Schuller stood at the edge. She held no weapon, but she had all the power she needed. He looked at her now, maybe finally understanding that this was the end of him. No escape. She created a wall of cold air between them and moved it toward him. Slow. She walked behind it.

"Please," he said. "Please. I just wanted to show the world something groundbreaking."

"How do you think Steve felt when he died?" she asked. "Lost out on the ice. Wandering, freezing. I'm sure he thought you weren't capable of such a thing. Probably shocked him to know that you would kill him for this." She gestured at the hole. The wall edged closer. He backed up.

"After learning that Bart was affected, you talked to him. What did you tell him? It didn't reassure him, that's for sure. He killed Jane and himself after that chat."

He started bawling then, sobbing. She ignored him.

"Beth, Bill, Jim, Alex," she said, counting on her fingers. "Four dead in the helicopter explosion."

"It was an accident," said Schuller, through choking sobs. "Andrew used too much—"

"I'll tell Bill's mother that," she said. "When I tell her you killed him."

The wall edged closer. Schuller tried to stand his ground, pushing a hand towards the barrier. A finger grazed the edge, and he screamed in pain, grasping his hand.

"Let's not forget Helena," she said. "She idolized you. You rewarded her with slaughter."

The wall edged closer. Schuller backed up, at the edge of the hole. He shook, and his crotch darkened as he pissed himself.

"And then there's Teddy," she said. "Who you made me slice open alive." A single tear rolled down her cheek. "You led Andrew down the path of madness, but Mike killed him, so I guess that one's not all on you. And Mike. The one who challenged you. The one who was strong enough to call out problems. You shot him as you ran, and he died. He deserved more. They all did."

"Please," he said, blubbering. "Just let me live. Let me see the ramifications of my discovery."

His heels skirted the edge of the hole, the wall of frozen air giving him no more room.

She shook her head at that, furrowed her brow.

"What do you think I will tell them, Doctor, when they rescue me?" she asked. "About what happened? About what we found?"

Schuller only stood there, his knees slightly bent, trying to resist the irresistible pull of the abyss.

"I will tell them nothing," she said. "I'm going to lie. We already know that no tests reveal the presence of the spark, and if they can't find it, I'm not going to tell them a thing. Why would I? So they can cut me open, like you wanted to? Or use me, for whatever dark purpose they might have?"

Schuller's lips quavered, his eyes watery.

"Your discovery is going to be buried," she said. "No one will know. You'll be remembered as the monster you are. No redemption. Now jump."

"Please—" he said.

"Jump," she said. "And it'll be fast. You'll die when you hit bottom. You could slow yourself on the walls, and last a little bit longer. Up to you."

"I—" he said, still just standing there.

"Fine," she said, dropping the wall of cold, and kicking him as hard as she could. Her ribs screamed in pain, but she didn't care. Schuller flew backwards, his arms windmilling, and he disappeared into the hole, bouncing off the sides until he was out of sight, the little light they had only illuminating the first ten feet. She could hear his yell, echoing up, until she didn't.

She heard no more sound from it. Maybe he slowed his descent enough to buy him a little more time, trapped in the darkness, surrounded by hard, hard ice. Maybe he was dead at the bottom. Didn't matter.

The ice would swallow him soon enough.

29

The helicopter came five days later. It gave her plenty of time to work out her story.

Most of the people departing for the winter had already gone, leaving McMurdo half-empty.

"So," asked Agent Russell, a recorder placed between them. "What happened?"

They sat in a small meeting room in McMurdo with a table and some chairs. They both had coffee.

"I was brought on to Tau as a medic, replacing Steven Kennedy, who died from exposure a few months into Tau's operation. I was friends with Mike Hale, the lead driller. He brought me on board. After a few days, I began to question the Dr. Ian Schuller's stability. We continued to make progress, but he was taking unnecessary risks to try and save time. I investigated the death of Mr. Kennedy, and found evidence that Schuller had forged his own psyche evaluation. By that time, we were close to mission complete, so I waited."

"I did some digging," said Russell. "And he pulled some strings with some contacts here at the base. Friends from college. Got him vetted for lead."

"I should have said something then, but I thought we'd be back soon enough, and I could bring it up then. We were all alone out there. I was new, worried."

She'd rehearsed all of this to herself, a hundred times. Not much else to do in those five days. Aside from taking care of the dead. Eating. Sleeping.

"Had you ever been out on the ice before?" asked Russell.

"No," she said. "I've done work on oil rigs. It's how I knew Mike. But nothing like this."

"It's always funny to me I'm stationed in Hawaii, which is heaven on Earth, but also here, which is, you know—"

"Hellish," she said.

"I'm sorry," he said. "Please continue."

"We reached mission complete," she said. "And things went downhill quickly."

"What exactly was Tau's mission?" he asked.

"With the ice warming, they got signals from hereto unknown cosmic rays, coming from deep in the ice. Schuller and his team thought this was evidence of undiscovered elemental particles. Building blocks that got lost along the way, is how I understood it. We were digging to find them. Record them, capture them, if at all possible."

"What did they find?" he asked.

"Nothing," she said. "By all accounts, they found nothing. None of the physical evidence, none of the monitoring devices, testing for every level of measurable science, turned up anything. Schuller was passionate, even obsessed, and finding nothing drove him insane. He kept pushing, kept pushing. No results, and most of us were ready to leave. As we neared the first bug-out date, Bart Sizemore lost his mind."

"He attacked Dr. Jane Morroll," said Russell, looking at his notes.

"Attacked and killed her," she said. "And later committed suicide."

"None of that was reported to us," said Russell.

"Schuller was responsible for communications to Mc-Murdo," she said. "I didn't think he would have gone so far to keep it from them. But it makes sense now. He was trying to cover everything up. Buy himself some time."

"Time for what?" asked Russell.

"Time for results," she said. "I was there when Bart—when he killed himself. Schuller had talked to him before he did it, before he attacked Jane. He had been having nightmares, hallucinations. I told him to rest, stay in bed, and he seemed to be getting better. And then Schuller met with him, and he killed Jane that night."

"You think he instigated something? Schuller?" he asked.

"Yes," she said. "But that was the beginning. Schuller had a new theory. That the particles they were looking for were now inside us. That they were rooted inside of some or all of us. And he wanted to pivot to study that."

"What evidence was there of that?" asked Russell.

"Both Bart and Teddy Ramirez were having visions and nightmares," she said. "He thought those were symptoms.

There was no other evidence."

"But they'd also both been on the ice for months," said Russell. "It could have just been cabin fever."

It wasn't cabin fever. They were inside them, just like they're inside me. Indivisible. Inseparable.

"He wouldn't listen," she said. "We were preparing to leave, everyone but Schuller, Helena Darrow, and Andrew Barthes. They were staying behind, holding on until the last second."

"And this is when the first helicopter arrived," said Russell, making more notes.

"Yes," she said. "Alex—I never got her last name. She was a marine too. The pilot."

"Alex Talbot," said Russell. "And someone placed a bomb on the chopper."

"Yes," said Mary. "Andrew, most likely. He was the chemist. Schuller later told me it was only supposed to disable the chopper, not kill anyone. But four died from the blast. Alex, Bill Norris, Beth Simmons, and Jim McTaggart. Helena warned me about the bomb, right before it went off. Mike and Teddy avoided the explosion, although Teddy had a minor injury, that I was able to patch up."

They healed him, Mary, healed him from inside. Could have healed from anything, even a live autopsy, if you gave him the chance—

"So that left you, Mike, and Teddy at Tau, with Schuller, Darrow, and Barthes?" he asked, his pen scribbling.

"Yes," she said. "We tried to arm ourselves, to find the radio. They booby trapped it, and it incapacitated Teddy. Mike and I thought they were holed up in Schuller's private lab, so we destroyed it with a tractor. They were waiting for us in the garage when we came back."

"Only Andrew and Schuller?" he asked.

"Yes," she said. "They had killed Helena. Schuller suspected that she had warned me. They cut her open while she was alive, looking for the particles. Schuller ate parts of her."

"Christ," said Russell. "And that's what happened to Teddy as well?"

"Yes," said Mary. She had rehearsed this moment the most. Her emotions were coming back, slowly. She would need all of them. "He had tied up Mike and Teddy, and was threatening to kill and torture Mike. He had a gun. He kept saying he needed me, needed my knowledge—"

She broke down then, her face squeezing, contorting in pain and sadness. She had looked in the mirror, watched herself do it. She covered her face, forced tears out, forced the emotion. She thought of Mike, her anchor to her emotions. It worked.

"We can take a break, if you want," he said. Perfect.

"No," she said, wiping her eyes with her sleeves. "I'm almost through. I'd rather do it all at once. He forced me to open up Teddy while he was still alive. Start chopping him up for him to eat. I slipped Mike a knife, and he cut himself free. Teddy died on the table, and both Schuller and Andrew turned on me. Schuller thought I had the particles inside of me. Mike got loose and attacked Andrew, killed him. I tried to get the gun away from Schuller in the chaos, but he grabbed it first, kicked me in my broken ribs. He ran then, firing shots as he left. One hit Mike, and killed him."

She had taken Mike's body outside. All of them. She didn't want to be alone with them anymore.

"And he fled?" asked Russell.

"Yes," she said. "I don't know. He took a tractor and drove off to the dig site. I tried to save Mike, but the bullet was in his chest. He died." She broke down again, and then collected herself.

"What happened then?" he asked.

"I tried to find Schuller, but he was gone. The first tractor was destroyed, and he had taken the second. I gathered what supplies I could, and waited. I barricaded all the outer doors to the main building, and five days later, the helicopter arrived."

She wasn't lying. She had driven the working tractor back from the dig site, after loading it up with supplies. She left the supplies in the main building, and then drove the tractor to the dig site. She left it there and walked back. With no cold or weather affecting her, it wasn't that hard. She worked out the story she would tell, and then barricaded the building to corroborate it.

"Did you hear anything from Schuller during that time?" asked Russell.

"No," she said. "I kept watch every waking moment. I didn't sleep much."

That was also true. She had slept much less since the spark. Three to four hours a night, and she was fresh and ready.

"We pored over the dig site, took a helicopter around the surrounding area. We found nothing. We suspect he jumped into the hole drilled into the ice. Either to kill himself, or out of some strange delusion."

"I'm glad he's dead," said Mary. "He deserved worse."

Russell looked at her, and only nodded. He studied his notes. It had been two weeks at McMurdo, waiting for the right people to be contacted and for the investigation.

"Your story checks out," he said. "As for your medical—"

Her stomach jumped into her chest. *There would be more tests, and they would find something, and they would cut her open, and find them inside her*

"For someone who went through the hell you did," he said. "You're as healthy as a horse. Nothing wrong. The doc said you're as normal as a human can be. So no worries there. Of course, we do have therapists at the ready if you need someone to talk to."

"I just want to go home," she said.

"Well, good news," he said. "Last flight out before winter is tomorrow, and you have a seat."

The flight was uneventful, filled with people finishing their contracts for the summer months, going back to civilization. Almost everyone looked hopeful. Everyone avoided her eyes, though.

They knew what she had seen.

30

"Keep breathing, Mary," said Doctor Larson. "You're doing great."

He stood between her legs, her ankles up on stirrups, his mouth and nose covered by a mask.

John stood beside her, holding her hand. She squeezed it tightly as pain ripped through her.

Mary's emotions had come back as strong as ever. It didn't happen all at once. It came in drips and drabs. The simple joy of meeting friends for coffee. Laughing at a movie. Lusting after some guy at a bar. In fits and starts, she felt things again. Right now, all she felt was terrified. She was having a baby, and she was terrified.

"Keep breathing, honey," said John, beside her.

In the flight home from Antarctica, to New Zealand,

to LA, to Chicago, she had thought she would never date again, that a human relationship would be impossible. She wasn't human anymore, and therefore human relationships weren't for her anymore. The spark had buried her emotions inside her somewhere. It was a simple impossibility.

But her emotions came back. She imagined the spark took them away because they wouldn't help her on the ice. She had needed to be detached, calculating to survive in a dangerous situation. But now that she was safe, her fight-or-flight mechanism no longer engaged, she would be safe to feel again.

And so they came back. But she didn't know if love was something she would feel again. Until she did.

The endowment that funded Schuller's research paid her a lot of money to keep her mouth shut about what happened there. She took it with a smile, enough money to do anything with. She stayed in Chicago and started a non-profit to help women who had miscarriages and stillborn births. She wanted to help people. They provided therapy, free medical care, and support for those women, and what would be a gesture of goodwill after so much death became her full-time job.

She just wanted to forget about Tau and everything that happened there. She kept moving, kept working hard, and she was rewarded with new work, new friends, and her feelings. And she met John. He was an OBGYN, working in their first clinic, pro bono in his off hours.

She didn't recognize the feelings at first, certainly not how she felt about him. But she talked to him, worked with him, and then ended up going out for coffee.

They dated. They moved in together. They got married.

She got pregnant.

"It's getting closer," said the doctor. "Keep breathing and get ready to push when I say so."

She focused on her breathing and looked up at John. He was focused on her, his face concerned. She squeezed his hand, and he let her, even as her grip was stone.

She never told him about what happened at Tau. She told him she was there, and that a lot of bad things happened. But she never told him about her abilities or how she survived. She never told him until the sadness hit. And then she had to.

Sadness had been the last thing to come back. She didn't know why. It just wasn't there for the longest time. She could watch the beginning of *Up* a thousand times, and feel not a hint of melancholy, not shed a single tear. Maybe her dog and pony show for the investigation used up her reservoir, and it took a long time to refill. She didn't know, but then it hit, and it hit her with everything.

It was two years back before she felt sadness. And then she felt it all at once.

They were having a quiet night at home, a rare one for both of them. They almost never were at home at the same time. They had been watching TV, her sprawled across him, a blanket over top of them. John was flipping through the channels. He had landed on poker and stayed on it only briefly, maybe thirty seconds. They came in just as the cards were being dealt and stayed long enough to see a single hand. Then he turned the channel to HGTV, to HBO, to whatever.

Then she was back in Tau, playing poker, everyone laughing, having a good time. And they were all dead now, except for her. Everyone at Tau, everyone who touched that place was dead, but no, not her, and Mike was dead, Mike who she almost settled down with, and Christ, she had to cut up Teddy, Teddy who suffered only because these things kept him alive the whole time, he begged for death, and she killed him, and Schuller deserved to die, but his eyes as he looked at her, and begged not to die, she killed him, she couldn't save them, all dead.

She had cried. Sobbing, her body wracked, shaking, uncontrollable. She cried for hours, and she couldn't talk. John held her, and waited for her to stop.

She had stopped, eventually, and she told him everything. He had to know. She loved him, and he deserved to know.

He had listened while she spoke. And believed everything until she talked about controlling the cold. She didn't blame him for that. But she finished the story, and then she showed him.

She had opened up all the windows in their Chicago apartment, in January. It was hovering around zero degrees that night, and the apartment got cold quickly, the wind howling. In short order, they were seeing their breath inside.

She had pushed it all out, and it was normal again inside. She brought it back, and pushed it away, at will. It was easy for her, because she had never stopped practicing.

It never rained on Mary. Never snowed on her either. The non-profit's office building was cold, from top to bottom, the AC always on, always too chilly. They had no control over it. Everyone brought an extra layer or used a heater, even during the summer.

Except for Mary. Her office was always perfect. Everyone said so whenever they spent time in it. She smiled and blamed it on the weird cooling system. But she kept herself comfortable. Kept herself safe.

He saw, and he believed, and he stayed. And he understood when she said she didn't want an ultrasound of the baby in her womb.

He had listened to her, her worries, her anxiety about having children, always a problem after her miscarriage, but now worse, different. What would their child be? The visions, the nightmares never recurred after returning, but she still remembered the ones from Tau. The insect creatures that came from inside her, her mind trying to reconcile the change that was happening to her. And she talked to him, and he listened, and he understood.

But she had still wanted a child. That never went away. It only deepened as she helped more and more women overcome their own fear and trauma. And so they tried, and they succeeded.

There had been no issues. She had an easy pregnancy, at least physically. She wasn't surprised by that. She stayed fit with no effort now. She could eat anything, never exercise, and never gain a pound. She never got sick anymore, despite seeing dozens of new people every day, as everyone else in the office rotated in and out, always fighting something. The spark had optimized her, and her pregnancy was no different. Another miscarriage no longer worried her. It was the birth itself that worried her, and constant countdown to the day they would welcome them into the world. Whatever *they* may be.

But as the date drew near, as they got closer, the ball of anxiety inside her stomach grew and grew and grew, and threatened to eat her whole. What would they see, on that tiny screen, as the kind Dr. Larson rubbed goo on her stomach and let them see inside? John tried to reassure her, tried to tell her, she looked human, despite what she could do, and so did he, and the baby would look the same. Any other differences—they could cross that bridge when they came to it. But she worried, worried, and he gave up, and told friends and family who asked that they wanted the gender to be a surprise, that they weren't worried about the health of the baby. Mary was as healthy as a horse.

And then it was time.

"Breathe in, breathe out," said John, his warm brown eyes on her, his easy smile right there, reassuring her.

"It's time, Mary," said Dr. Larson. "Focus on your breathing, and—push!"

She pushed, her baby inside her, wanting to get out, her whole body telling her it was time. She pushed. The pain was there, was everywhere, enough pain to push that terror away. There was only the baby now, and she pushed.

"Good job," said the doctor. "Breathe, breathe, breathe, and now—push!"

She pushed, and she was being ripped apart, and she squeezed John's hand, and she focused on her breathing. She breathed, and she pushed as hard as she could.

"Almost there, you're doing great," said Dr. Larson. "One more time should do it. Breathe, breathe, breathe, and push, push hard!"

The sweat dripped down her forehead, her heart was racing, and she breathed, and she pushed, and the pain, and then relief, a vacuum inside of her, and she knew it was out, and then enough of her mind came back to worry again, to feel anxiety to feel terror *oh god please let them be normal.*

Dr. Larson stood between her legs, working, holding the baby in his arms, cutting the umbilical.

The baby wasn't crying. The baby wasn't crying. She didn't hear anything. She couldn't see she couldn't see.

"Where's my baby? Is everything okay?" she asked, her voice as loud as she could muster on her short breath.

Larson stood up, holding the baby. She couldn't see his face, couldn't see his reaction. Couldn't see the baby, only his hands, his arms engulfing it. The nightmare was there, right there, floating in her mind. It was a monster, wasn't it? *They would take it from her, it wasn't human, it wasn't—*

"It's a beautiful baby girl, Mary," said the doctor, and carried the baby to her. He presented her and Mary took her in her arms. She saw her for the first time. She was perfect, her eyes open and breathing normally. She was pink, with a mop of shocking blond hair on top of her head.

"Look at that hair," said John, from above her shoulder.

"She's amazing," said Mary.

And she was.

31

It was hot in this particular part of Georgia, the hottest part of the summer. Except not for Mary, and not for Evie, who held her hand on this wooden, worn porch. They were comfortable. They always were.

Mary knocked on the door. They were expected, but she always felt nervous knocking on a new door. A remembered anxiety returned. She looked down at Evie, and Evie smiled back. She always did.

The door opened, an elderly woman on the other side, a gentle smile on her face. She was short, and somewhat bent, but she used nothing to assist her in walking. She moved fast for her age. A thick Southern accent came from her.

"You must be Mary," she said, not a question. She extended a hand, and Mary took it.

"Yes," she said. "And this is Evelyn."

"Well, hello Evelyn," she said, craning over to look her in the eyes. "How old are you?"

"I'm five," she said, the sheepish smile still on her face. Evelyn reached out her small hand and the woman took it.

"It's nice to meet you," said the woman. "My name is Eleanor, but you can call me Ellie. Everybody does."

"Nice to meet you, Ellie," said Evelyn. "And you can call me Evie. We both have E names."

"We certainly do," said Ellie. Ellie straightened back up, as much as she could.

"Why don't you two come inside?" she asked. "I've got some biscuits in the oven, just for you."

She walked down a narrow hallway, through the old cracker house, into a modest kitchen, every possible space serving a specific purpose, most of them serving two or three. Decades of efficiency honing the kitchen into its finest point.

"You two can sit right here," she said, pointing at a kitchen table surrounded by four chairs. "It's where all the business in the house gets done. And by business, I mean a bunch of chattering."

Mary and Evie sat down at the table, solid wood chairs and table, old, but still working. Mary could describe everything in the kitchen like that, except the fridge, which seemed new. Even had a screen in it.

"Y'all want anything to drink?" she said. "We have tea, water, Coke—"

"Water would be great," said Mary. "For both of us."

"I want Coke," said Evie.

"I don't know," said Mary. "You've already had enough

sugar today."

"It won't hurt her," said Ellie. "They're the tiny ones, you know. I drink too much of them if I don't get the tiny ones."

"Ok, one Coke," said Mary. "I want you to thank Ms. Ellie."

"Thank you, Ms. Ellie," said Evie, as Ellie placed a tall glass of water in front of Mary, and a tiny can of Coke in front of Evie.

"You're very welcome," said Ellie. She looked into the small window of the oven, a dim light hanging inside. "Biscuits need a few more minutes. I don't trust timers. They won't tell you what the biscuits need. Only your eyes can do that."

She sat down next to Mary and leaned back into the chair. Evie began to color, taking a coloring book and some crayons from a small backpack she wore, a picture of She-Ra on it.

"I'm sorry it took me so long to call you," said Mary. "To visit you."

"Oh, darling," she said. "You didn't need to come at all. I don't expect visitors. Not like I live on main street or anything. And to come, all that way, from Chicago—"

"I promised him," said Mary. "And it may have taken a while, but I try and keep my promises. And it was only fair that I see you face to face."

"I appreciate it," said Ellie. "I do. I'm always happy to make my biscuits for new people. Spread the gospel, so they say."

"You taught Bill how to cook?" asked Mary.

"I did," said Ellie. "I had all boys. Six of 'em. And Bill was the only one who learned how to cook. He was the youngest. Might have had somethin' to do with it. All his brothers got to everything else first. Cooking was the only thing left for him. Took to it like a duck to water."

"Everything he made for me was great," said Mary.

"His pa, God rest his soul, hated it at first," said Ellie. "Told me no son of mine belonged in a kitchen. Men worked outside the home, women inside of it. Told me that he wouldn't allow no such thing, not in his house."

"What did you do?" asked Mary.

Ellie smiled, and reached over to Evie, covering her ears with her hands. "I told him that if he ever wanted fucking dinner again in *his* house, that boy could learn to cook if he wanted."

Mary laughed, loud and hard, and Ellie let go of Evie's ears. Evie looked around confused for a moment and then went back to coloring.

"Turns out a boy could learn to cook, as long as his momma didn't take no crap," said Ellie. She smelled the air, her nose up. "Time for them biscuits to come out."

She pushed herself up, out of her chair, and walked over to the oven, grabbing mitts that had seen a thousand biscuits. She opened it and pulled out a baking sheet covered in golden brown mounds of dough, each steaming. The smell was incredible.

"That smells good, mommy," said Evie, her eyes still on her coloring.

"You're right, it does," said Mary.

Ellie put the sheet on the counter, and then turned to Mary.

"Forty-five seconds," said Ellie. "They rest forty-five seconds. Butter or honey?"

"Which do you suggest?" said Mary.

"I suggest both," said Ellie, smiling again. "Butter on one half, honey on t'other."

"Sounds good to me," said Mary. "Right sweetie?"

"Yep," said Evie, coloring still. The time passed, and Ellie cut through three biscuits, dropping six halves on three plates. She slid them onto the table. She grabbed a stick of soft butter from its spot on the counter and a little jar of honey from the pantry.

"Butter is from the store," said Ellie. "But the honey is local."

They each slathered the hot biscuits with butter and honey silently, Mary making Evie's for her. They ate. Mary ate the side with butter first, and then the honey. The biscuits were perfect. Warm, gooey, yeasty, fluffy, and the butter and honey suited them.

"Bill was right," said Mary, finishing her last bite. "Yours are better."

Ellie laughed, loud, like Mary had before.

"What do you think, Evie?" asked Mary.

"They are deeeelicious," said Evie.

"Well, I got the opinion that matters the most," said Ellie. "Is it okay if Evie helps me make the next batch?"

"Sure," said Mary. "Evie, do you want to help Ms. Ellie make some more biscuits?"

"Yes!" said Evie. "I can help, I can help."

"Will you grab that stool in the corner for me, Mary?" asked Ellie, and she did, and Evie stood on it.

"Anything else I can do?" asked Mary.

"Help yourself to another biscuit," she said. "You're nothing but skin and bones."

She grabbed another biscuit, doing the same as the first, as Ellie showed Evie how to make her biscuits. Within a few minutes, another batch was in the oven. They stared into the oven together, Ellie craned over, Evie right at the oven window, looking in.

"They'll start to brown, and just right when you see the first one start to turn dark brown, you take them out," said Ellie. "So just watch. You say when."

They sat in silence, as the biscuits baked, and Evie kept her eyes peeled.

"Now?" asked Ellie, testing her.

"No, not yet!" said Evie. "Nnnnnnnnnnnnnnnnnnnow!"

They jumped to their feet, and Ellie grabbed the biscuits out of the oven.

"Now count to forty-five seconds," said Ellie. "Can you do that for me?"

"Yes!" said Evie. She started counting. Mary took it in, enjoying the smell of more biscuits. She could eat a dozen more.

Evie hit forty-five, and Ellie took one of the fresh ones and cut it in half.

"Butter or honey?" asked Ellie.

"Honey!" said Evie.

"How'd I know you'd say that," said Ellie, dripping the local honey on top of the biscuit, handing it to Evie. "For your hard work."

"Thank you, Ms. Ellie," said Evie.

"No, thank you," said Ellie. "Can you do another thing for me?"

"Yes!" said Evie, smiling up at Ellie.

"I want you to go to my tomato plants out back, and I

want you to pick off every caterpillar you see, and put them in this bucket. Can you do that?"

"Yes!" said Evie. "What do tomato plants look like?"

"They look like vines," said Ellie. "Do you know vines?"

"Yes!"

"Vines with little red fruit," said Ellie. "Be careful with those caterpillars. I've got some tweezers you can use. Don't use your fingers, no matter what they look like. I'm gonna talk to your mom for a little while. I'll give you a quarter for every caterpillar you find."

"Really?" asked Evie.

"Really," said Ellie.

"Is it okay, Mom?" asked Evie.

"Of course," said Mary. "Don't go past the tomatoes, okay?"

"I won't," said Evie.

"They're straight out that door," said Ellie, pointing. "Can't miss 'em."

Evie ran out, the bucket swinging in one hand, the tweezers in the other. The screen door creaked shut behind her.

"That was very sweet of you," said Mary. "You don't need to pay her."

"She'll be lucky to find one, to be honest," said Ellie. "It's not caterpillars that kill the tomatoes. I'm just not very good at growing them. Everything else works out just fine. Never the tomatoes. I've tried everything."

Ellie sat down next to Mary again, preparing another biscuit to eat.

"How did Bill die?" asked Ellie, buttering her biscuit, her voice losing all the joy that was in it before.

"What did they tell you?" asked Mary.

"Not much," said Ellie. "They gave me a fair share of money to hush me up, and I bought that fancy fridge with it. Wouldn't give me answers anyway, so might as well take the money."

"How much do you want to know?" asked Mary. "It's not pretty."

"I want to know," said Ellie. "My youngest born dying before me. I want to know."

Mary told her.

Ellie didn't cry, only went quiet for a while.

"I'm sorry," said Mary. "I'm sorry it took so long."

Ellie's lip quivered, just for a second, and then she collected herself.

"You came," said Ellie. "That's more than anyone else did."

"He told me to tell you, that your biscuits made it to Antarctica. New world record, he said."

Ellie cried then, tears rolling down her cheeks. But she smiled.

"Don't move," said Ellie, and she got up again, walking out of the kitchen, returning two minutes later, a stack of white, ripped envelopes in her hands. She laid them out on the table, each of them a letter, with a picture of Bill included, him holding a biscuit, one of his momma's.

"Brazil. New Brunswick. Northern Alberta. Glasgow. Japan. So many places," she said, pointing at each picture. "Wherever he went, he made my biscuits. He took a part of me across the world, even when I wouldn't go. Couldn't fly. Scared to death. Antarctica was the last continent. All seven. World record."

They looked at the pictures.

"I'm glad you were there for him, at the end," said Ellie. "Some people don't get that. He's in a better place, with his pa. I'll see him."

They talked for a while, about everything. They got along.

"It's getting late," said Ellie. "And I need to rest these bones. Let's go collect your daughter. See how many caterpillars she's caught."

Mary followed Ellie outside, to the little garden she had. A variety of plants grew out of neat little sets of dirt. A hanging hose dripped nearby. Evie was easy to see, right near the tomatoes.

"Oh my God," said Ellie, rushing up next to her. "I don't believe it."

The tomatoes weren't dying, like Ellie had suggested. They looked amazing, fully grown, snaking around the cage support, thick, full, bright red tomatoes everywhere.

"I thought you said you couldn't grow tomatoes," said Mary.

"I can't," said Ellie.

"They looked sad," said Evie. "So I helped. See?"

Evie walked over to the last tomato plant. It looked sad, like the state that Ellie suggested. Small and wilted, off color. Evie looked at it, and sunk her hand into the dirt, her tiny fingers digging in. She closed her eyes, and the tomato grew, shooting up, getting greener, fuller, the fruit growing before their eyes, thickening. She opened her eyes, pulled her hand up, and the plant was there, perfect.

"I don't believe it," said Ellie, touching the tomato, seeing if it was real. "She's a miracle."

Evie smiled up at her mother. Mary looked at her, the

same easy smile as her father. Ellie could keep a secret. She *hoped* Ellie could keep a secret.

"You're right," said Mary. "She is."

Acknowledgements

Thank you to my wife Kim, for her patience and support, and my team of beta readers: Andrew, Matt, Megan, Yousef. Thank you for reading. And thank you to John Carpenter, for The Thing.

About the Author

Robbie Dorman believes in horror. Underneath is his third novel. When not writing, he's podcasting, playing video games, or petting cats. He lives in Texas with his wife, Kim.

You can follow Robbie on Twitter @robbiedorman

His website is robbiedorman.com

Subscribe to his newsletter at robbiedorman.com/newsletter

Enjoy Underneath?

Sign up here to be notified about Robbie's next novel!

robbiedorman.com/newsletter